INSCRIPTION

Winner of the Eludia Award

Hidden River Arts offers the Eludia Award for a first book-length unpublished novel or collection of stories by a woman writer, age 40 or above. The Eludia Award provides $1000 and publication by Hidden River Publishing on its Sowilo Press imprint. The purpose of the prize is to support the many women writers who meet with delays and obstacles in discovering their creative selves.

Hidden River Arts is an interdisciplinary arts organization dedicated to supporting and celebrating the unserved artists among us, particularly those outside the artistic and academic mainstream.

Who can say what life was like in ages past?
W.G. Sebald, *The Rings of Saturn*

*This notebook is begun today, the 18th of October, 1998,
by Aubrey Evans in the fifty-fourth year of her life.*

An empty book is like an infant's soul, in which anything may be written. It is capable of all things, but containeth nothing. I have a mind to fill this with profitable wonders.

—Thomas Traherne, *Centuries of Meditations*

The archaeologist is dead, and I am released from my promise to him, my silence about Marina and her manuscript. She began writing it nineteen hundred years ago, during her banishment from Rome to the island of Ponza; her voice should be heard at last.

Now, on this autumn morning in the northeastern United States, at the very end of the twentieth century, it is time; and indeed what better day than today, the feast of Saint Luke, patron of doctors, icon-writers, and bookbinders?

And so I have opened this big blank book, I am writing in it after all these years. I bought it long ago in a Florentine bindery, seduced by the chestnut calfskin, the blues and greens of the marbled endpapers, and the smooth creamy pages. It has waited, empty as an infant's soul, and I did not know why, but it was for this.

The blank book embodies centuries of craft: rounding, backing, covering, stitching, all the work bookbinders have perfected ever since the codex, in an obscure evolution, began to supplant the scroll. The mysterious birth of the codex was in fact the subject of that conference in England where, five years ago, I first learned of Marina's manuscript.

The conference was held not far from where I was born and grew up. Also attending was an archaeologist I'd met at previous paleological and papyrological gatherings. One day he took me aside between two lectures and made an extraordinary statement. He told me he had found something even more spectacular than the Vindolanda tablets, something that would change all we thought we knew. He valued my opinion, and wanted to show me, but on condition that I said nothing about it to anyone.

I was curious, and agreed. He lived a couple of hours away from where the conference was being held, and so I took a train, and the usual complex feelings welled up as I watched the green and hazel landscape unscrolling past the window. It happened every time I went back to England, this painful recognition of how much I loved it, and of why I had needed to leave. In the archaeologist's town, I found his nondescript block of flats, climbed to his door, rang the bell, and heard him sliding bolts and turning locks before he let me in.

There in his study, on his everyday desk, lay a black object, nearly square, about eight and a half by nine inches, and about two inches thick. Its carapace was of leather so old as to be almost fossilized, and from it trailed two long leather straps. They were tied around it all this time, he told me, keeping it closed, protecting what was inside. And with gloved hands he gently lifted the top layer and folded it outwards, so I saw it was the cover of a book: a parchment codex of many pages, nested one within the other, gathering upon gathering. And I saw, very faint but still visible, the writing on the first page.

"I believe," said my host, "that this is an original, first century AD manuscript."

Of course I thought he was quite mad. So few, and such fragmentary, bits and pieces of writing are extant from that distant time in the Greco-Roman world. Especially in codex rather than scroll form. Parts of early codex books have been found; but the oldest known complete ones discovered so far, the gnostic books of the Nag Hammadi Library, date from the third and fourth centuries.

He gave me gloves and a magnifying glass and invited me to take as long as I liked to examine the handwriting, while he busied himself with papers in a corner of the room. I fumbled in my bag for the reading spectacles I had just started to need, pulled the gloves over my fingers, and began by looking closely at the book as a whole. The leather cover was not attached to the spine; a loose strand of thread still clung to the folds of the gatherings, but the stitches holding the pages together had come undone. A few leaves had probably been lost. As I pored over the writing on the first page, and then on several different pages—turning them with the utmost delicacy—excitement cramped my heart. After only an hour, I was certain he was right.

"Take more time," he said, "to be sure; and because you might never see it again."

So I studied the ancient parchment for a long, unforgettable afternoon. It was a warm June day; if I surfaced for a moment I became aware of traffic sounds and birdsong coming through the open window; inside the room, dusty with books and papers, there was the occasional dry cough of the archaeologist. I tried to stay calm enough to concentrate, to do the task all my paleographic work had been leading towards. Every moment spent learning to decipher the ancient letter shapes of the Roman cursive alphabet came to bear now, as I scrutinized the manuscript's competent hand. And all along I was marveling, hardly believing it possible that these were the very ink letters another living woman shaped, so long ago, with the articulation of her wrist, and her warm fingers on the pen. For the scribe was indeed a woman, as the first line made clear.

Letter by letter I teased the words apart from one another, worked out where one ended and another began, until I had the opening of her text: *marina britanna flaviae domitillae libraria in pontia insula has membranas incipit . . .*

With a shock I recognized the words *pontia insula*: they snagged at a tangle of emotion almost thirty years old.

Ponza, the island off the Italian coast, with its pale buildings and white cliffs; the place where in five days my life changed, when I was a very young woman. I had returned home to England, afterwards, with two books about Ponza, and their mysteries and contradictions sent me burrowing into the comforting stacks of the nearby university library. Deep among the endless shelves of volumes I escaped my sorrow, submerging myself in the island's ancient past. I learned about the Roman tunnels, and the remnants of villas; I studied the story of Domitilla, Ponza's co-patron saint, whose church I had seen, but only from the outside. There was a controversy about whether she really existed. According to hagiographic legend, she was a Roman Christian exiled to the island in the first century. Some ancient historians did mention a Flavia Domitilla sent to Ponza; but others said she was banished to a different island. I traced this old puzzle through the knots of argument; the modern historians, like the ancient ones, drew opposing conclusions. There were no answers, but at least I had been distracted from the painful meaning of Ponza in my own life.

Now, all these years later, here was this manuscript by a woman calling herself Marina the woman from Britannia, scribe of a Flavia Domitilla, and beginning her book on the island of Ponza.

The codex was real, I touched its leather cover and its parchment pages, but I do not know where it is now. The archaeologist never told me where he had found it, or how it had survived against all odds; never revealed where he kept it, beyond assuring me that the place was safe, and the temperature and humidity were properly controlled. All I have of the oldest surviving codex from the ancient Western world is the photographic copy he made for me.

He was determined to breach every kind of protocol and keep the manuscript secret until he had finished preparing a scholarly edition. But he needed a paleographer, and one who specialized in ancient Latin scripts, to interpret and transcribe the codex. He knew my work and he liked my being unaffiliated with the gossipy world of academia. Before I left his study that afternoon, he made me solemnly promise again not to tell anyone about the manuscript. Although I knew this was wrong, I understood his fierce desire to possess, for a little while, this tangible piece of the past. Indeed, from the moment I saw the codex, I wanted it myself.

I have never seen it again. He ushered me out of the study and locked the door. It was early evening; over a glass of sherry in his living room, I agreed to his conditions. As well as keeping the manuscript a secret, I had to stay in England while working on it, apart from visiting Italy if necessary for research. I had to suspend my American life.

Later, I arranged for long-term care of my house and garden back in America. The private school where I taught had offered me a sabbatical not long before; I told them I was ready to take it, starting that fall semester. Then, feeling strangely foreign in my native country, I rented a flat in Oxford.

I worked almost non-stop to decipher Marina's handwriting. I visited Ponza for the second time, seeing it now through Marina's eyes. Once or twice I asked the archaeologist if I might clarify a difficult reading by consulting the original, but in vain. When my transcription and translation were ready, I sent them off to him. Afterwards I heard from him only occasionally, when he wanted to discuss this or that detail; and when he told me that laboratory analysis of the ink and parchment of a tiny piece of a page supported a date of the late first century AD. Then, this past February, he suddenly died, his edition still unpublished and the manuscript still unknown. As soon as I read his obituary in an archaeological journal, I begged permission from his survivors—a sister and a nephew, as he was unmarried—to study his papers. They refused.

And so, with the archaeologist's death, I consider myself freed from my promise, though I still cannot reveal his identity. Perhaps someone, some day, will publish his unfinished edition of Marina's manuscript, and his name will be common knowledge. Perhaps the original codex will be found safe in its unknown hiding-place.

In the tales of early Irish saints, precious books are saved through miracles. A careless monk once dropped Saint Ciaran's gospel book into the lake on Inis Angin, Hare Island, where it remained for a long time, until one day a cow waded in to drink, and the strap on the book's cover caught on her hoof. She brought the gospel out of the water with her; the pages were white, dry as bone, every letter clear.

It is almost as miraculous that Marina's manuscript survived so long, although its letters are far from clear, and the sense is often elusive. But I know her story intimately now; I have read her lines over and over, and I have read between them.

In the pages of this blank book I will copy out my translation of Marina's manuscript; and between her words I will interpose my own, gathering the fragments I have found, the profitable wonders. It is old-fashioned to write by hand these days, but I enjoy the intimacy of the fingers with the pen, and the strokes of the pen on the paper. I relish the movement across the empty leaf, and the fatness of the unused block of pages under the side of my writing hand.

Marina's manuscript will be the warp, and my miscellany the weft, of a *textura*, a fabric I cannot yet name or imagine. But I do know that the final text, however tightly woven it may appear, will really be a net, an openwork of filaments from one knot to another, with empty spaces between.

The academics often said I was on the edge of serious scholarship; well then, I claim once more the freedom of the borderlands. I have been scrupulously accurate in rendering Marina's words, but I will not impose any such discipline on mine. I no longer have the energy for the academic niceties, I'm not interested in confining myself to scholarly jargon, and I cannot promise to keep myself decorously out of the picture.

Marina of Britannia, scribe to Flavia Domitilla, begins this notebook on the island of Pontia, on the tenth day before the kalends of June, in the year of the consulship of the emperor Domitianus Caesar and his cousin Titus Flavius Clemens.

There, I have written the first words on the first page. As if I were still in Rome, making an inventory of new books or a tally of copied manuscripts. As if everything were the same. But it is all changed. I am no longer in the city, in the wing of the imperial house high on the Palatine hill. I am on Pontia, this barren rock. That illustrious household I was part of for so short a while is now destroyed. Titus Flavius Clemens, consul this year, has been killed by the emperor, his own cousin. His wife Flavia Domitilla, the emperor's niece, has been banished to another island, Pandateria. I sit here on this terrace, just after daybreak. I have mixed water into the dry ink, and filled the inkwell. Tilla is still asleep: Tilla, the girl who draws trouble to herself, and others into her trouble.

This parchment notebook can no longer fulfil its destiny. The household doctor gathered his medical notes and his recipes for salves and infusions, scribbled on various wax or wooden tablets and scraps of leather. He asked if I would write them all in one place. Flavia Domitilla gave her approval, and instructed me to buy a durable parchment notebook of good quality. But Flavius Clemens was killed before I could begin. The household broke apart, and the doctor vanished, his notes with him.

Now all I have are these empty pages. Yet I seek words to write, although I can no longer call myself scribe to the lady Flavia Domitilla. Her island prison Pandateria is only just visible, faint and far, from the point where the lighthouse stands.

We sailed from Ostia yesterday. Into the water quickly they put us: washed us out of Rome. A river boat down to Ostia. Then a ship to the islands. There were three guards: two for Flavia Domitilla and the five Christians. One just for Tilla and me. The wind was strong. The sea was angry. The sickness overwhelmed me, and the fear of the fathomless waters. That fear has been with me ever since I was a girl in far-off Britannia, and I was cast out alone onto the open sea. Yesterday the waves threatened to swallow us and I dreaded the invisible tentacles, stretching to drag us down. One of the Christian women stayed with me. She comforted me until we reached this island. Our guard made Tilla and me disembark with him. The ship went on to Pandateria with the Christians and Flavia Domitilla and the baby.

I am here on this rock in the sea with a girl I hardly know.

I was glad to find a home in the house of Flavia Domitilla. I wanted an end of traveling from place to place. Now I may indeed have an end of it. I may be here until I die. Even if I were free to leave this island, the only way is by crossing the sea once more.

⁓

Islands are self-contained, easy to understand . . . paintings are really islands. The theater is an island. A book's an island.

—Betsy Wyeth

To read an island, it is best to begin with circumnavigation. And some traces of the past are only visible from the sea.

It's five years ago now that, while working on the manuscript, I returned to Ponza. It was July; I took the boat tour around the island, the same loop I had taken long before, in very different circumstances. The boat begins by skirting the promontory called the Punta della Madonna, one of the arms of the semi-circular bay protecting the port. The *barcarolo* shows his passengers where the Roman harbour used to be, and the remains of a Roman jetty, then guides the boat alongside the buff, ash and ochre volcanic cliffs. High on the tip of the headland, poised like a seagull, is the white cluster of the cemetery: it overlies part of a ruined Roman villa, almost certainly the one where Tilla and Marina lived in their banishment. From the boat below, the strata of the clifftop's edge are seen in striped cross-section, sheer as a cut cake. There's a distinct manmade layer, now giving purchase to the roots of the trees that shield some of the graves from the wind.

Only from the sea can you discern the faint shadow of long-eroded steps in the rock, where a stairway once led from the villa right down to sea level. There at the foot of the cliff is a complex of caves called, picturesquely but inaccurately, the grotto of Pilate. These caves were Roman fish pools; the boat noses into their dark openings, under the low, arched ceilings with sparse remnants of decoration in shell and mosaic. Still visible beneath the water are the partitions, which could be lifted, allowing the fish to swim from one prison into another.

As the boat moves around the island, it comes to a natural arch of rock rising out of the sea. The boat passes under the arch as through a city gate, then rests for a while in the clear shallows: the sea constantly moves in little peaks and dips, and these movements catch the sun, so there is a net of gold over the blue-green water. A web of reflected light is cast across the sand of the sea floor.

Time suddenly folds in upon itself: the boat made the same pause near the arch, rested in the same net of gold, when I, or rather, we, took the same tour all those years ago. The palm of his hand was hot on the skin of my thigh.

The sea is not always so calm, the barcarolo says; storms batter Ponza and the other islands in this scattered archipelago: Zannone, Palmarola, Santo Stefano, and Ventotene.

Then the boat slips once more into the sheltering curve of the harbour, with the light-washed clustered houses, the square Bourbon fortress-turned-hotel, and the cupola of the church.

Ninth day before the kalends of June. Third day on Pontia.

This is exile. But I have my writing box. In it I have my pens, I have my full inkwell with its tight stopper and lid, and I have brought everything to this outdoor terrace. Once again it is early morning. Now I lift the inkwell's lid, remove the stopper, take one of my reed pens, dip it, and write. The familiar movement of my hand calms me, and the steady procession of the letters, although I have no list to make, no book to copy.

This villa is high above the sea. The colonnaded terraces step down the cliff towards the water. Old cracked stairs lead from one level to another.

Far below, boats slip out of the harbour, setting off for the morning fishing. I can just see the coast of Italy on the horizon. Behind that distant shore is Rome, where even a consul, an emperor's cousin, is not safe.

When we arrived here, the winds were unfavourable for using this harbour. We approached the island from the other side. As the boat drew close, I saw we were entering a semi-circular bay with steep cliffs falling sheer down to the sea. It looked so like one of the coves of my childhood, the one we called cove of the moon, that for a moment I did not know where I was.

We disembarked. Tilla and I were taken through a long tunnel, dark and dank, under the rock. Then up steep lanes and steps before we reached this house at last.

We stood in the shabby atrium, and Tilla's composure broke. She fell to the ground and crouched there, rocking and wailing. I clenched my teeth against her fear, and against my own.

This parchment is smooth; this notebook is well made—I bought it from Secundus, the maker whose work I prefer. He has matched the hair sides and flesh sides of the skins, so a pale flesh page lies beside pale page, yellow page by yellow.

Eight days before the kalends of June. Fourth day on Pontia.

Yesterday Tilla paced up and down, inside, outside. Or stayed in her room. Glauca the housekeeper gave us a room each. I asked Tilla if she would like me to keep her company at night, as a nursemaid or governess has always done, but she refused.

To her, and to all who see me, with the blue-etched indelible patterns of my people around my wrist, I am a barbarian. Although I am a free woman of twenty-three or twenty-four years old, I am held almost as low as a slave girl. And in her eyes I am like one.

In my eyes, Tilla is foolish and dangerous. We are here through her fault.

It is windy outside today, even under the colonnades. Here inside this musty, windowless cubicle, sitting on the bed, I write by a feeble flame. The book and lamp rest on a shaky little table. The old-fashioned wall paintings of satyrs chasing nymphs are faded, the floor's herringbone tiles are cracked.

My traveling chest stands in the corner: a gift from Cosmas, before he disappeared. Deep inside are the things I brought from Britannia, long ago. They have journeyed with me all these years: the cloth my mother made, and, wrapped inside the cloth, the mirror. I do not often look at that bundle because of all the sorrow in it. But I keep it with me.

I am lost. I have no place. We are not safe here. The commander of the garrison said he would be watching us. No leaving the grounds of the villa, no visitors unless approved. One wrong step and he will send up his soldiers, with their brutal hobnailed boots, their lethal swords, their power to kill us in an instant.

Tilla's aunt asked me that terrible day to look after the girl. But I am helpless, and I have no comfort for her, no comfort for myself.

Seventh day before the kalends of June. Fifth day on Pontia.

The hours are long.

I often sit here, on the third level down, in the shadow of the colonnade. I look out over the water. The gulls ride the air. They cry with the same voices as the gulls that called to me when I was a child. The rocky cliffs are not green with grass like those of my home. But here, as there, small bushes are flowering bright yellow, and the salt smell is the same. I have been breathing it in deep. The house is steeped in saltiness.

It is too cold and damp in winter, says Glauca. Too windy. No one wants to live here once summer is over. You will long for this heat when those days come, she says, laughing.

Surely we will not still be here on this island when winter comes?

Tilla and I barely speak, closed up in our separate miseries.

The procurator of the imperial property lives in another house near the harbour. Glauca and her husband look after this one, with a cook and a few slaves. Everything in the house is old, of fine quality but shabby: cracked marble and warped wood.

There are ghosts. In the night I seem to hear the exiles of past years walking up and down the damp corridors. Glauca, stooped and bony, remembers them from so long ago: even as a little girl she worked in this house. She has hoarded all their stories of desperation and loneliness and forced suicide. She wheezes out these miseries with glee. Is she waiting for Tilla and me to die too?

Once Caligula asked a man returned from a long exile how he used to spend the time. To flatter him the man replied: "I constantly prayed to the gods for what has in fact come to pass—that Tiberius would die and you become emperor." At which Caligula, thinking that the people he had exiled must likewise be praying for his own death, sent agents from island to island and had them all slaughtered.

—Suetonius, *Gaius Caligula*

An apartment on Ponza is ideal for spending a holiday in an untamed, uncontaminated, natural setting, in complete freedom.

—Modern tourism brochure

I stayed at the Hotel Torre dei Borboni, not the rather shabby *pensione* of my first visit twenty years before. (It had closed down, but I would have avoided it anyway.) My room had a deep window embrasure because of the thick defensive walls, and sitting there I could see the Punta della Madonna headland, now corrugated with vineyards in bright green terraced rows, and, at its far point, the cemetery.

The cemetery is white on white, even the stairs between the levels are white; dazzling in the sun. Whitewashed pathways squeeze between the tight-packed chapels and the walls full of burial slots like drawers, each with a name and sometimes a photograph attached. The surnames of the dead are the names on island shops and doorplates—Mazella, Coppa, Scotti, Sandolo. There is also a memorial to four antifascists, from distant northern Italy, who were among the hundreds interned on Ponza under Mussolini, and who died there, far from home. Later, Mussolini himself was held on the island for a few days.

Ponza has been a place of exile for a very long time. The Roman villas on Ponza, and on Ventotene (once called Pandateria), were seaside retreats for the emperors, but were also useful for the banishment of their out-of-favour relatives. The ruins of the enormous villa on the headland lie not only under the cemetery but also beneath the terraced vineyards and under the Bourbon tower. Bits of the villa can be seen above ground: parts of the retaining walls, and, almost obscured by vines, a segment of masonry in the diamond pattern of *opus reticulatum*, work like a net.

The high, rocky headland thrusts itself into the sea, a sea so much more than blue that there is no word for the colour of it: a sea that is purple and turquoise and azure and wine and cobalt and green. This was a delightful spot for an emperor on holiday with all his retinue. For an exile, banished from his or her community, it was a place of bitter punishment. And at any time death could come by order of the emperor: death by the sword, or by starvation, or by opening one's own veins in the bath.

Sixth day before the kalends of June. Sixth day on Pontia.

I am sitting in my usual writing place, leaning against a pillar, looking out over the harbour and the rest of the island. The houses of the rich Romans are scattered up and down the scrubby hills. Perhaps some of those families know Tilla's family. But they are forbidden to have anything to do with us. The soldiers keep them away, Octavius the cook told me. And the commander made it clear: we may not leave the villa grounds.

Octavius was taking eels one after another out of a squirming bucketful. He killed and gutted each one deftly. They are reared by the hundreds in the fish pools below the house. With them we will eat a few chickpeas.

I fear the soldiers. I cannot forget the commander's brutal face.

Fifth day before the kalends of June. Seventh day on Pontia.

Tilla and I have been speaking a little more to each other. She drifts aimlessly through the almost-empty rooms and along the quiet colonnades. In that house high on the Palatine hill, over-looking Rome, there was a slave for every task. Some washed clothes, others pressed and folded them, and one boy's whole job was to whet the kitchen knives. My ten days there were not enough to learn the names of the many gods and ancestors in the atrium, nor of all the living inhabitants. There were guest rooms, dining rooms, bright mosaic floors, three kitchens, laundry rooms, and rooms I never saw.

All the world was gathered there: silks from China, jewels from India, alabaster cups from Egypt. There was even a woven basket from my own land. To Flavia Domitilla it was just another object from a distant place in the tales of her dead father, Quintus Petillius Cerialis. He was in Britannia in the days of our great Boudica, whose armies nearly killed him. Later, when Flavia Domitilla was a child of about eight, he was governor there. That must have been near the time I was born. So the father of kind Flavia Domitilla was an oppressor of my people. And her mother was the daughter of Vespasianus, whose army stormed our hill fortress and killed my grandfather and so many brave warriors.

I have seen baskets like that being made. I have seen the basket-maker's old husband, grey and quiet, by the stream in the valley on a misty morning. He scurried to cut his lengths of reed and willow as if gathering straws for a nest. His wife worked them with twists and braids of her own design. The basket in the Roman house was not one she made, but tight-knit and strong, like hers. Its woven spirals were songs to me. Sometimes I lifted it to my face and breathed deep of its grassy scent.

And now, my writing box on my knees to support the pages, I am sitting as I sat when I wrote letters for Flavia Domitilla. The last time was not many days ago. The baby was at her breast. She

fed him herself, as she had fed her six other children. Greedy little thing, she said, tenderly, in the midst of her letter—I almost
wrote that down. As she bent her head to him, her high-piled
curls wobbled and began to fall. In the letter she dictated that
day, she told a friend that she trusted Hermas, Grapte and
the other Christians who visited her house. She said the evil
rumours about Christians were not true. I wonder now if that
letter somehow reached the emperor.

At the end she gave the baby to the nursemaid, and wrote a final
note herself. I blotted, folded, and tied the letter. I began to leave
the room.

She told me to sit down again.

Was she going to send me away from her house? She took the
baby, laid him on her shoulder, and patted his back, prompt-
ing a sweet little belch. Then she smiled at me and said my
work was good. She said the tutor Quintilianus taught only
the two older boys, whom the emperor Domitianus had
named as his heirs. So she wanted me to give writing lessons
to her fourteen-year-old niece, the younger Flavia Domitilla,
known as Tilla.

The rest of that day I walked light-footed, gave thanks to whatever fortune had brought me into that household, whatever
gods were smiling on me at last. I saw with new pleasure the animal paws of the tables standing firm on the floor, my own san-
dals treading those opulent mosaics, the candelabra festooned
with good-luck phalluses, the walls painted with red panels and
a creamy froth of undying flower-garlands.

Here at last was a house where I could belong.

But now I am banished to Pontia. And now Tilla too has lost
everything that was familiar.

Now my book comes to hand, and the two-tone parchment scraped free of hair; some papyrus too, and a jointed reed pen. Then we complain because the ink is thick and clots upon the nib; but when water is added, the cuttle-ink darkness disappears, and we complain that the reed tube is scattering diluted blots everywhere.

—Persius, *Satire III*

Marina's manuscript is indeed, as the archaeologist said to me, even more spectacular than the Vindolanda writing tablets found on Roman Britain's northern frontier. One of those postcard-like slivers of ancient wood is well known for bearing the earliest handwriting almost certainly by a woman. At about the same time as Marina was writing in her notebook on Ponza, Claudia Severa on the other side of the empire was dictating, to a scribe, an invitation to her friend Lepidina. They were both wives of Roman officers stationed in Britain. She asked Lepidina to come and celebrate her birthday, sent good wishes to Lepidina's husband from her own husband and son, and then added, in her own hand, these words:

sperabo te soror vale soror anima mea ita valeam karissima et ave.

I shall expect you, sister. Farewell, sister, my dearest soul, as I hope to prosper, and hail.

So few women's voices speak to us directly from the ancient world, so few are heard even indirectly through the men. The words Claudia Severa dictated to her scribe are a rare testimony; these she wrote herself even more so. Here is one woman speaking to another, calling her *soror*, sister, and *anima karissima*, just as Italians today say *carissima* to a beloved girl or woman. This woman's few handwritten words salvaged from the centuries are so precious; how much more so is Marina's entire book.

On Ponza, I gazed across the vineyards, trying to imagine the villa's walls and rooftops there instead of the green vines; trying to see Marina sitting on a terrace with her writing box, her *theca libraria* as she calls it, containing her pens and ink.

When she began setting down her own words, she did not know where the writing would take her. As I do not know where this writing will take me.

She dips her pen in her inkpot full of ink made from carbon, gum Arabic and water. (Though ink could also come from the *sepia*, or cuttlefish.) The words for pen, *calamus* or *harundo*, both mean *reed*; and the pen might be made of an actual reed, or of a metal such as bronze. Marina has both kinds. She writes on parchment, called *bicolor* by Persius because the side where the animal's hair grew is yellow and pitted with hair follicles, while the underside that lay against the flesh is white and smooth.

When I was a child at school, I had a scratchy metal-nibbed pen with a wooden shaft, and I dipped it into ink kept in a little glass inkwell that sat in a special hole in the desk. A groove carved into the desk held the pen when I stopped writing, as long as I settled it there carefully so it didn't roll down and splatter ink on my exercise book. Then came fountain pens, which drank from the squat bottle of Quink; and pens with replaceable cartridges, easier to use but still messy; I always had inky fingers. I struggled to learn the art of varying the thickness of the strokes by tilting the nib, making a pattern of thin upstroke and bolder downstroke within the larger pattern of the letters themselves. It was easier, if less artistic, to use the ballpoint, and then, later, the felt tip, the roller ball, and the gel pen, like this one I am writing with now.

Throughout my time at school and college, we wrote our essays by hand. Then my mother bought me a typewriter when I embarked on my master's degree. She thought, we both thought, that it would see me through the master's and my doctorate as well. When I had to give up the doctorate, my mother took the typewriter and marched through the house with it, out of the back door to where the metal dustbins were; she elbowed the lid off an empty dustbin and dropped the typewriter with a terrible cacophony of rattling keys and sliding carriage and the clang of metal on metal. She crashed the lid back on, came indoors and said,

"This is the end of all my hopes for you."

Fourth day before the kalends of June. Eighth day on Pontia.

Octavius told me today that I have been keeping the right date. He saw on the public calendar at the harbour that this is the fourth day before the kalends of June. It is a festival day. That explains why the soldiers were here.

I had just stepped out on the terrace at the edge of the cliff, and looked down at the small jetty far below. A boat was tied up there. As I watched, four soldiers came out from the fisheries. Sun glinted off their shoulderplates. They carried buckets of fish and joked about the feast they will have tonight. I could not move. My heart was pounding. As the boat drew out to sea, one of them looked up and caught sight of me. Then I stepped back quickly, crouched down, but I heard them laughing, threatening to come up and visit us.

The metal and leather, and the harsh laughter, instantly bring back the house in Rome, the emperor's guard bursting into Flavius Clemens's study—I hear in my ears again his cries of No! Please, no! They pulled him out of the room and through the atrium, his feet in exquisite red shoes dragging across the floor. He called for his wife—I pressed against a pillar, the marble cold on my cheek—Flavia Domitilla ran to him—the whole household began to gather at the sounds, as they had gathered early that morning for the daily prayers invoking the protection of the gods and ancestors. All heard the captain of the guard announce:

Your wife Flavia Domitilla is relegated to the island of Pandateria by order of the emperor.

There was silence, the air thick with fear. The gods had abandoned us.

Flavius Clemens shouted that he was Caesar's cousin, his wife was Caesar's niece, his sons Caesar's chosen heirs. The captain proclaimed:

Our Lord Domitianus Caesar purges his house of atheists who prefer the foul superstitions of Jews and Christians to the holy and ancient rites that sustain the city of Rome.

The girl Tilla rushed forward to Flavius Clemens, shouting, Forgive me, forgive me.

Why? What was her fault towards her uncle?

They dragged him away, and one guard stayed, holding back his wife Flavia Domitilla as she tried to run after them. She writhed in his grip, and screamed: a long, terrible sound.

Her steward Stephanus went towards her and took her from the guard, supporting her as she almost collapsed. The guard relinquished her, laughing.

Soldiers are here on Pontia too, nearby, with their swords. The emperor has only to lift a fingertip and send a message across the water, and the soldiers will kill us. His hatred reaches us even here on this island. Tilla, who was at first spared from being punished with her uncle and aunt, brought his wrath upon herself as well. And on me.

If only I had stopped her.

Third day before the kalends of June. Ninth day on Pontia.

For the first days here Tilla never sat with me to eat. Glauca brought the meals into a small sitting room but Tilla would snatch up her food and take it somewhere else. Now for the last day or two she has eaten with me, although she eats very little.

I am pleased to have her near. And yet I am still angry, as if we are both trapped in that audience with the emperor, when she risked everything, and lost.

The day before the kalends of June. Tenth day on Pontia.

Over and over, those last days in Rome torment me. I resist them. Perhaps if I yield and let the memories come, my mind will be free. Perhaps if I write them down, they will leave me in peace.

My work has always been to write the words of others—a letter dictated by a mistress, a book needing to be copied. Never words of my own beyond a note to a pen maker or to a seller of parchment. But everything is different now.

There was no time to mourn the consul. We swiftly buried all they had sent back of him, his decapitated body, without the head. Flavia Domitilla was given two days to prepare for her exile on Pandateria. There was chaos. Guards in the corridors. Slaves separated, most to be sold, a few not. The whole household had to leave the palace. Tilla and all the children except the baby were going to a small house owned by Flavia Domitilla. What would happen to me? Not a slave, I was free to leave. But I had nowhere to go.

On the second day, around noon, Tilla grasped my wrist with her long fingers, snatched the case of scrolls I was carrying and laid it aside. She whispered, Come with me quickly; say nothing to my aunt.

If only I had held her back, if only I had not meekly let her pull me through the door that led to the emperor's part of the palace. But that is why she chose me, because I was new in the household. I did not know how to stand up to her. She ran ahead and I hurried after, through a labyrinth of corridors, up and down flights of stairs, stepping into gardens warm with the sun and then plunging back into the chill of stone and marble. I followed, I did not stop her, even when her sandal broke. She picked it up and carried it. As we ran across a graveled courtyard I saw blood on the sole of her bare foot. Then we came to the emperor's quarters. The white-liveried doormen admitted us. Doors and anterooms, gold and red and green, and mirrors everywhere. I followed the smears of her blood on the marble floor.

That is enough.

The kalends of June. Eleventh day on Pontia.

I shall finish what I began to tell.

At last, we were admitted into a small room. A man with a heavy chin lay on a richly cushioned divan. Quite ordinary-looking, much balder than his portraits. There was a Robbers game board on the table, and standing beside it a little boy all dressed in crimson. He had a grotesquely small head. The emperor seemed to be teaching him to play. Two other men watched and laughed.

Tilla stepped forward, stood in front of the emperor with one bare foot, holding her sandal, and begged that her aunt might stay in Rome with her seven now fatherless children. I shrank back against the wall. He put down his game piece.

He said, It is decided. Flavia Domitilla is banished to Pandateria. She will be my guest at the imperial villa there.

Tilla pleaded with him, crushing her sandal with both hands against her breastbone. She asked how he could do such a thing.

He looked at the other men. He would show them how he dealt with impudence. And in a quiet voice he said Tilla too needed some time away from Rome, in a secluded place. Another island, where he also had a house: the island of Pontia.

Smiling, he added: And you and your aunt can swim back and forth to each other.

He knew what we did not yet know, that Pontia and Pandateria are far apart. The water is wide.

Then he looked at me and said, almost as an afterthought:

That blue-etched, green-eyed beanstalk goes with you. No one else, no slaves. One chest each, only the belongings you can fit inside it.

He said, looking at Tilla again: You will be stripped of everything.

The men laughed.

He called a secretary and had our sentence of banishment written down on a tablet, as calmly as if he were ordering his dinner.

The guards marched us back down all the corridors, almost dragging us, my legs weak, in the smell of sweat and leather. One man's fingers locked round my upper arm, biting the flesh. The bruises are there still. At our door, a boy ran to fetch Flavia

Domitilla. She walked across the atrium, a jug in her hands. The
guards read her the tablet and watched with mocking smiles as
her face changed. She dropped the jug, and it shattered on the
floor. Oil spilled out, pooling across the mosaic eyes and mouths
of Orpheus and Eurydice.

*The vessel touched at the island of Pontia ennobled long since as the
place of exile of the illustrious lady Flavia Domitilla who under
the Emperor Domitian was banished because she confessed herself
a Christian; and Paula, when she saw the cells in which this lady
passed the period of her long martyrdom, taking to herself the wings
of faith, more than ever desired to see Jerusalem and the holy places.*

—Jerome, letter to Paula's daughter Eustochium

When I went back to Ponza, knowing of Marina's manuscript,
I tried to look beneath the layers, the accretions of time. Roman
water cisterns have been incorporated into the fabric of some
buildings, and rooms built two thousand years ago have become
cellars for old wine bottles and torn fishing nets. On the way
down to the church from the hotel I noticed that the long shallow steps under my feet were made of a mixture of shells, gravel,
stones, and fragments of Roman marble.

I went into the parish church of Saint Silverio and Saint Domitilla, which I had not set foot in when I was on Ponza before;
I had only read about it back in England, afterwards. Inside I
found a statue of Domitilla, and also a wall painting of her with
many other saints. There were wallet-sized holy pictures of Domitilla's statue superimposed on a Ponza clifftop, with the blu-
est sea behind. She is a tall slim girl in flowing robes and a red
cloak lined with ermine. There is a girdle around her hips. In
one hand she holds a lily for virginity, in the other the martyr's
palm. On the back of the little card are the words of a hymn to
Saint Domitilla, beloved virgin, precious to God, protectress of
Ponza, fragrant white rose, red rose, she for whose altar the island's maidens weave pious garlands of lilies.

Every dictionary of saints defines Domitilla (if at all) in a different way. Some say there were two exiled early Christians called Domitilla, some say there was only one, and some cast doubt on there having been any. She was officially dropped from the General Roman Calendar of saints in 1969, for lack of evidence.

A leaflet from the church tells one version of her legend. According to this largely unhistorical tale, she was a relative of Domitian's who at the end of the first century consecrated herself as a virgin to Christ. But a young Roman, Aurelianus, fell in love with her and sought her hand in marriage, persisting even when she refused him over and over. At last the infuriated Aurelianus colluded with the emperor in having her exiled to Ponza for her faith; even there he pursued her, and sent loose-living women to draw her into sensuality, but they became Christian too. Aurelianus finally organized a festival and forced Domitilla and her companions to take part. During the celebrations he suddenly dropped dead while dancing. His brother accused Domitilla and the other women of murder by magic, and took them to Terracina on the mainland, where they were burnt alive.

This story is part of a complex hagiographical romance created sometime in the fifth or sixth century. But it was not spun out of nothing. Much earlier, there was already an established memory of Domitilla's exile on Ponza, her "long martyrdom" as Jerome says. When his friend Paula visited Ponza in 385 AD, the island had been "ennobled long since" as the place of Domitilla's banishment.

Now Marina's manuscript reveals the kernel of these half-remembered legends, these layered encrustations.

Every year on Saint Domitilla's feast day, May 12th, the parish priest of Ponza leads the traditional candle-lit procession to the ancient rooms under the church where the islanders have always believed she lived, the "cells of Domitilla," perhaps the very same ones Paula saw. I wanted to visit them, and I went from the priest to a restaurant to a fisherman to a relative of his and then to that relative's aged aunt, who said the person with the key was off the island for an unknown length of time. And in any case, I was told, nothing could really be seen of the cells because they were filled with rubble from the collapse of the buildings above.

I met a woman who had gone inside the rooms when she was a little girl; she saw carvings of Christian symbols and a crown. She remembers how the villagers used to bring roses and pile them there for Domitilla.

Four days before the nones of June. Twelfth day on Pontia.

I am sitting on the low wall in the inner courtyard today, sheltered from the wind, and in the shade. My inkpot is balanced beside me on the uneven stones of the top of the wall. The wind is warm but strong, the seagulls cannot hold their course. We shall have rain, says Glauca hopefully. She has invoked the gods every day, fearing for her thirsty vegetables and herbs.

(Later.)

Tilla came into the courtyard then and saw me writing. She stopped and sat on the stone bench a little distance away. She studied the ground, bent down and pulled savagely at the weeds growing in the herringbone brick pavement. We were silent for a while. Then she asked, Why are you always writing, writing? Is it a letter?

And I told her, no, it is not a letter. Or a letter to myself, perhaps.

Another silence, and in it a small change happened between us.

Then Tilla said, Do you remember the text I chose when you gave me that writing lesson?

I laid down my pen. I do remember. It was the first—and only— lesson we had. We began in a room off the peristyle. A scented breeze blew in between the pillars and made her restless. I gathered up my tablets and styli and book of writing exercises, and we went outside. We sat on a cushioned bench, near the fountain I liked best, the one with the dolphin. The poppies were bright splashes, and a few early roses had opened. I started unrolling the book of practice pieces, but Tilla took it from me. She passed over quotations from Virgil and Livy. She chose some lines from Ovidius Naso's *Lamentations from Pontus*. How strange that she should pick those poems of banishment, written in a place named for the Greek word "sea," like this island. Almost as if she glimpsed the future. Although Ovidius was on the shore of a far distant sea, at the edge of the world.

Today, in this very different courtyard, we groped together for the words until we had them right. He wrote how in his exile he wished for wings, how he longed to

> *fly through the thin and yielding air, and soon*
> *I'd see below the sweet ground of my Rome.*

She repeated them sadly. But that day in Rome, I said to her, remembering, You told me you wanted wings too. Wings to fly far, far away from the city.

I added, It is often said, be careful what you wish for.

That was unkind. She was silent. Then she picked up my pen and asked if she might try her hand. So I gave her the scrap of parchment I use to test my ink. She wrote: Flavia Domitilla. She said, That is my name, the name my aunt and uncle gave me when they took me in, the same name as hers, to show I belonged to that family. Who am I now? What family do I belong to? My uncle is dead. And even my aunt may not be alive any more.

She released the pen from her thin fingers, stood up, and walked quickly away.

During that first lesson in Rome, as she copied the words of Ovidius, she had tried to dash across the tablet with the stylus, impatient when the wax slowed her down. I watched her thin face leaning over the work, her rather pointed nose, another stylus almost, hovering over the wax. She did not like making the same words over and over. It was the best way to learn, I said. Surely she wanted to be able to write pretty thank-you notes for her wedding gifts one day? She jumped up and went inside. I was left alone on the bench by the fountain. That was only two days before the death of Flavius Clemens.

Now, left alone again, I think of what the old nurse Baucylia in Rome told me. It was soon before she died suddenly, in her sleep. A kind fate. She never knew of the murder of Flavius Clemens, the exile of his wife, and the scattering of the seven children she had cared for from birth. She told me Tilla came to the household as a little girl about three years of age. Her parents, relatives of Flavius Clemens, had both died. There were no other family members who cared to take her in.

Such a scrawny scrap, said the nurse, who was bathing Flavia Domitilla's youngest child as we spoke. The very baby now exiled with his mother to Pandateria. Baucylia said little Tilla asked over and over when her Mama and Tata and her own nurse were coming back.

She settled down in the end, Baucylia said, lifting the baby's fat little arms and legs, molding his knees and ankles to make him grow tall and straight.

She said, I burned that filthy toy she held so tight, a doll made of rags. Little by little she grew used to me, and to her new family.

She added, Tilla is fourteen, she should be married soon. But she will not hear of it. What will become of her?

I know the answer now, here on Pontia. My burden, that is what she has become. After the soldiers dragged us back from the emperor's quarters, Flavia Domitilla wept over her niece in bitter grief. But it gave her some comfort to know that Tilla would not be exiled alone. She begged me to look after the girl.

Third day before the nones of June. Thirteenth day on Pontia.

Today Tilla asked me how I became a scribe.

It is so long ago, about ten years, since my first lessons in writing as a girl in far Britannia. The tutor Cosmas had dark hair and brownish skin. He understood our language, and spoke it too, though in a way that made my brother and me laugh. But he frightened us when he told how in his land the earth shook one day. Even great stone buildings fell down, and his wife died in their crumbled house. We did not understand how the earth could shake. Now I have felt it myself.

He took a metal thing like a twig, warmed it in the flame of a lamp, and with the pointed end he made a scratch in the dark wax of a tablet. Then with the blunt end he pressed the wax flat until the mark disappeared, as if it had never been there.

You can smooth your mistakes away, he said. He gave each of us a slim stylus and a wooden tablet with an empty field of wax.

The writing things felt good in my hands.

First we learned to write our names. This was soon after I had been given my name as a woman. He said, we do not have exactly that name in Latin. But we write this: M A R I N A. He wrote those letters on the tablet. Then his warm hand came down over mine, guided it. Our hands together made the letters again. He told me to copy while he helped my brother. Slowly, crookedly, fist clenched around the stylus, I did so, as carefully as I could. I wanted to show him I was no child but a young woman of thirteen winters. I copied and copied, the stylus steadying, the lines of each letter more firm. There in the wax was my name. Those marks meant me.

The lesson over, my brother ran off to find the other boys. I went down the steep cliff path to the sea cove. From the innumerable smooth pebbles of many colours, I chose a grey one from above the tide-line. It was dry and round. It was the hard kind, flecked like marble. This was the best stone for the slingshot. It fitted my palm. I took a piece of the soft white chalk that lay under the grass of the clifftops and in fragments on the beach, and I wrote my name as the tutor had shown me. I had to use my fingertip to rub off some of the letters, as they were not straight enough. I wrote them again. At last I was satisfied with the way the white lines of my name looked. But the chalk smudged too easily.

From playing with pebbles I knew how to draw on them with the semi-translucent flints. I searched for a good sharp one, and made letters: I scratched M A R I N A as deeply as I could. Then I traced it again with the chalk so it showed white. My name was on the stone. I held it, looked at it. I was proud of my writing, but a little afraid. What if this stone fell under a malign power? Was there a safe place to nest it in?

Not on the beach, for the winds and waves to buffet my name to nothing. I turned my back on the sea, faced the cliffs. There were crevices and crannies in them, many quite deep. Birds sometimes hid their eggs there. I began climbing right above a particular rock at the foot of the cliff, the rock we called Horse's Head. High up, I found an empty hole, a little tunnel, warm and dry. I slipped my hand in, and laid the stone inside. I asked the powers of the earth and sea and sky to guard it well for me. Then back down on the beach I studied the cliff and memorized the place exactly. Some day I would climb up again and find my stone.

Learning to write was hard—letter by letter, syllable by syllable, line by line from poets and philosophers. Yet I found satisfaction in slowly mastering the shapes of the letters and the meanings of the words. Also in the teacher's praise: I wanted to please Cosmas. I never dreamt writing would one day come easily to me. I never imagined I would learn book-copying calligraphy, letter-writing hand, and Greek writing too, and possess styli and tablets, and parchments, and pens of reed and bronze. Or that my destiny would bring me so far from home, to places of hot sun, with olive trees whose leaves turn over silver in the wind.

Writing soothes me, gives me solace here on this island locked in salt waters, with the wide sea all around, a palisade against departure.

———

To such a degree, indeed, did the teaching of our faith flourish at that time that even those writers who were far from our religion did not hesitate to mention in their histories the persecution and the martyrdoms which took place during it. And they, indeed, accurately indicated the time. For they recorded that, in the fifteenth year of Domitian, Flavia Domitilla, daughter of a sister of Flavius Clemens, who at that time was one of the consuls of Rome, was exiled with many others to the island of Pontia in consequence of testimony borne to Christ.

—Eusebius of Caesarea, *Ecclesiastical History*

At this time the road leading from Sinuessa to Puteoli was paved with stone. And the same year Domitian slew, along with many others, Flavius Clemens the consul, although he was a cousin and had to wife Flavia Domitilla, who was also a relative of the emperor. The charge brought against them both was that of atheism, a charge on which many others who drifted into Jewish ways were condemned. Some of these were put to death, and the rest were at least deprived of their property. Domitilla was merely banished to Pandateria.

—Cassius Dio, *Roman History*

I have attempted to prove elsewhere—and the most recent studies agree with me on this point—that the Flavia Domitilla . . . exiled to Pontia is not the same Flavia Domitilla that Dio records as having been exiled to Pandateria.

—Marta Sordi, *The Christians and the Roman Empire*

Three women bore the name Flavia Domitilla: Domitian's mother, sister, and niece: the first two were dead before he became emperor and the third married Flavius Clemens. Early Christian writers . . . argued for a fourth, niece of Flavius Clemens (i.e. daughter of a supposed sister) and have won acceptance from some scholars. She can safely be discarded.

—Brian W. Jones, *The Emperor Domitian*

These fragments encapsulate the contradictions and the controversy. The memory of a Domitilla exiled to Ponza goes back at least to the early 300s, when Eusebius was writing; but the non-Christian sources he mentions have not survived. Instead we have the very different tale of Cassius Dio. And of course both Eusebius and Cassius Dio wrote long after the event.

Was Flavia Domitilla wife or niece of Flavius Clemens? Mother of seven children, or young virgin? Christian or Jewish? Banished to Pontia or to Pandateria? The apparent contradictions can be resolved if there were two exiled women of the same (not unusual) name, one the wife of Flavius Clemens and one his niece, each banished to a different place. Some scholars, like Marta Sordi, have chosen this solution. But many others hold Eusebius and Jerome guilty of a series of errors and a confusion of islands. They believe with Brian Jones that the younger Domitilla, the consul's niece, can safely be discarded.

When, back in England after my initial visit to Ponza, I encountered this mystery, first in the books I brought back from the island and then in the library, I followed its tangled strands with curiosity and excitement, glad to have something to sink my teeth into, something to help me forget what was happening in my own life. I traced the complex arguments, and I loved the way the trail looped back and forth between domains often kept apart: history and hagiography, early Christianity and ancient Rome. I enjoyed the different personalities of the scholars who wrote about these elusive Domitillas; I followed their alliances and feuds. I became absorbed in the passions of obscure writers in rarely consulted books.

The more I encountered contradictions between this expert and that, the more I perceived how important it is to keep the net open, to let unimagined ideas and people and lives slip through, to let them emerge from the dark pools of the past. Marina's manuscript not only settles the controversy; it shows that the real story is in the gaps, in the interstices of what the historians and the hagiographers knew, or thought they knew.

Many of those who pronounced firm opinions in favour of one conclusion or the other will not see her book; they are no longer in this world. Do dead scholars discover, across the Styx, the answers to the questions that consumed them in life? Or are there other mysteries to solve there, matters of the heart and soul?

I may find out soon. I am only fifty-four; but one apparently small physical symptom is, it turns out, connected with a web of other symptoms of which I was unaware.

We have left undone those things we ought to have done. Although I have not been to a church service since childhood, except for the occasional wedding or funeral, these words echo within me now. There is indeed so much I have left undone in distant England.

And there is no health in us.

The nones of June. Fifteenth day on Pontia.

It is over, but this writing betrays my still-shaking hand. Today, suddenly, a clanking and shouting and rattling of hobnailed boots came up the rock-cut stairs from the villa's boat landing far below. Nearer and nearer. The slave girl Chloë and I left the bucket of water and clothes and scrubbing brush in the court-yard. She ran to the kitchen, I hurried to find Tilla, told her we must hide in some corner of this rambling house. She straight-ened her back, she said, No. No hiding. I will not show them any fear.

The soldiers, three of them, burst in laughing, panting from the stairs. We were alone, with only old Glauca nearby. Her hus-band Philemon was somewhere outside among the vines. The cook and the slave boys and girls were in distant parts of the house, as I wished I were. We stood there. My heart was drum-ming so I could hardly breathe. I smelled the wine on their breath and coming from their skin. One was hardly more than a boy, and like his comrade he followed the lead of the short-est and most aggressive man, whom they called Minimus and who began the taunting. They swayed a little, and made as if to unsheathe their swords—both kinds. They stared at Tilla. They could see she wanted it, they said. They stared at me. We don't believe that old wives' tale about a green-eyed gaze being unlucky, they said. Gaze all you like. See how ready we are, they said, and fingered their priapic bulges. They were almost play-ful, yet the more menacing for that.

Then an extraordinary thing happened. Tilla looked them in the eye, coolly, one by one. She held her head high and said, Does your commander know how you are dishonouring Rome? And do you know that I am of the emperor's blood and family?

She spoke with such authority, and remained so calm. I hardly know how it happened, but they went away. She seemed com-pletely unafraid. I am ashamed of my own fear. I hope she did not see me tremble.

We sat down on the rickety chairs. She is just a girl, wrists as thin as reeds. Now, for the first time, she told me she is sorry that she involved me in her plea to the emperor, sorry that I am here on Pontia because of her. The knot of anger inside me has loosened a little.

But I am afraid the soldiers will come back.

Sixteenth day on Pontia. Eight days before the ides of June.

I write in the last light of day: the breeze is growing stronger. Although it is June, the evenings are cool. It must be the same for Flavia Domitilla on Pandateria. The palace guards taunted her as she prepared for exile: That sea air turns cold, they said. Leave your fine silks behind, take your woolens, your heaviest cloak. Leave the makeup, the hairpieces—no one will be looking at you except cicadas and jellyfish.

But Flavia Domitilla was never a woman who troubled about her appearance. And surely she has other anxieties now, there across the water on Pandateria, with the baby. She has lost her husband and her home, her other children are far away, and she cannot even reach Tilla here on Pontia.

Nineteenth day on Pontia. Vestalia. Five days before the ides of June.

This is the day of the Vestals, as we learn from Octavius's report of the harbour calendar. He sees it every morning before he comes to the villa.

Instead of the chaste priestesses tending Rome's flame today, I think of the Vestal Cornelia, and of her appalling end four years ago. I should have remembered her fate in April, before I joined the household of Flavius Clemens. Her death should have warned me to have nothing to do with the emperor, his family, or the Palatine hill. I should have heeded the whispers about uncanny omens and strange disappearances. I should have listened to the rumours of the emperor's whims, the way he crucified slaves just for copying books he did not like.

But I was dazzled to think I could be part of the household of a consul and live in a wing of the imperial residence. Flavia Domitilla needed a writer and copyist, and I needed a new position. It seemed a most fortunate destiny.

I was among the crowds who watched Cornelia's carriage go through the streets of Rome. The drum beat slow doom. The people in the streets were somber and quiet. And there she was, Cornelia the Vestal, exposed to the world in her holy robes and headdress. She screamed in anguish, begged Vesta to save her, called on all the gods, cried that she was innocent, that she had not broken her vows of chastity.

A very old man next to me wept. He had never in all his long life seen this terrible punishment carried out on a Vestal. But Domitianus was adamant for the ancient penalty. They say he even condemned Cornelia in her absence, gave her no chance to speak for herself.

The procession was slow. The priests walked solemnly, heads bowed. I saw her face, the naked terror in it. Things I wanted to forget came into my mind: the last night in Britannia, when I lay strapped to the ceremonial couch. The dreaminess from the herbal drinks was penetrated by a sickening fear as I waited for the morning, for the launching of the boat. And I knew nothing would hold the morning back.

Cornelia's procession stopped near the Collina gate. The crowd gathered around the entrance to the underground room. There's a bed in it, went the whisper, and a lighted lamp, and food and drink. The priests helped her out of the carriage: she had stopped her terrible cries now. They led her to the top of a portable flight of stairs placed so she could walk down into the hole with dignity, facing forwards. She stood there for a moment, as if she were freely choosing. Then she began to go down the steps, tall and straight. Suddenly her robe caught on the rough wood with a ripping sound. One of the priests stepped towards her to help. She lifted a hand fiercely, as if to say, do not touch me, I am still a Vestal. She unsnared the fabric herself. Near the bottom of the stairs she seemed to crumple, she fell, and then we could not see her any more.

They laid the boards over the pit, like a lid on a box. Then the spadefuls of soil began to thud on the wood. One long scream came up from underneath. The trumpeters played more loudly as the earth was piled high, beaten down, covering everything. We all gradually dispersed until no one was left. Except Cornelia, under the ground, alive.

Four days before the ides of June. Twentieth day on Pontia.

Tilla is unwell. She has stopped her walks and pacing and staring out across the water towards Pandateria. She lies in her room long hours.

I think she is ill in body because she has suffered so much in mind and heart. Today I tried to ask her how her health was in Rome, before everything happened. It was normal, she said, but with a strange hesitation in her voice.

Why did Flavia Domitilla lay the care of this girl on me?

We found [the skeleton of] a sixteen-year-old fisherman, his upper body well developed from rowing boats, his teeth worn from holding cord while he repaired his fishing nets.

—Sara C. Bisel, *The Secrets of Vesuvius*

On Ponza, as in so many places, early Christian history nudges up against the secular history of ancient Rome; these two kinds of history are in reality inextricable. Saint Domitilla, and the islanders' longstanding belief in her, coexists with the ruined villas, traces of aqueducts and remains of Roman amphorae. Looking for evidence of such stitchings-together, I walked up and down the steep lanes of Ponza over and over, as if I could walk myself into the past.

I walked so much that I broke a sandal, and had to ask where to find a cobbler. They told me at the hotel to follow the curve of the bay around to the village of Santa Maria. This meant going right through the main town in the harbour and then through tunnels the Romans had cut under the bay's rocky promontories.

Four men working on their nets showed me where to find the cobbler's shop at the top of a flight of whitewashed stairs. Halfway up, a pair of shoes waited for the cobbler's attention. The door was closed; near it stood a simple wooden kitchen chair, under which a black-and-white cat gnawed on a whole fish. I knocked, and in a few moments a little woman emerged from a level below and came up to open her shop; she was ancient, and so small in her long black dress; her tiny hands like bird claws and yet still strong. As she examined my sandal I sat on a chair and stared around the room, at the piles of fishing nets in the corners; the photos on the walls of her as a young woman, working on nets with her husband, and stitching sails; the shoes everywhere. She agreed to mend my broken strap. A few days later, I went back for the repaired sandal, and she quoted a price so ridiculously low, less than the cost of a cappuccino, that I realised she could not have raised her fees in about fifty years. I had no money small enough, and she fished the change out of a frail cloth purse that was once an elegant evening bag.

We talked a little. The festival of the island's main patron, San Silverio, had taken place shortly before my arrival on Ponza; she said she preferred the olden days when the statue of the saint was draped in gold and jewels for his procession, the way it was done for centuries. The priests now forbade this as too pagan.

I asked if she had always lived on Ponza, and if she ever wanted to leave. She said, of course it is crowded in summer, and cold in winter with a chilly wind off the sea. But she has never wanted to leave.

"*Perche? E il mio paese*," she said. *It is my home.*

Then, with that disconcerting Italian swiftness, she asked whether I was married or had a *fidanzato*. I told her I had no husband, nor even *fidanzato*, and I was a free woman. *Una donna libera.* And this ancient little person, who herself seemed a living embodiment of history, whose life had been so long and so full of gruelling labour, said, "Freedom is good, yes. But you seem a little sad."

"Oh no, I am not sad at all," I assured her. "Ponza is so beautiful, and I am working here, I am doing historical research."

She looked at me.

"I can read your eyes," she said, "And you are sad."

And so I left, neither admitting nor denying it.

The fishermen were still mending their nets, the nets hanging down against a wall, the line held in the men's teeth, their hands swimming deftly in and out with needle and mesh stick, making knots and openings.

About the fourteenth day before the kalends of July. Around the twenty-eighth day on Pontia.

I have not picked up my pen for a while. I have been helping Glauca clean some of the unused rooms here. Not that it is especially necessary: no visitors are expected. But it is something to occupy the time.

We are in high summer, and the hours and the days are at their longest and most scorching. When evening finally comes, it is only a little cooler. But how welcome is this small relief. I am sitting in the courtyard in the last of the daylight, waiting for the breeze off the sea.

As I write now, I find I have missed doing this writing. I have neglected this notebook because I have been so cast down. Any words I wrote would have been lamentations. Today, the peace of the evening, the promise of the breeze, and the tiredness of my body bring me some calm. I return to my parchment companion.

The air is darkening. I hear the squeaks of the evening's first bats flying to and fro. Soon I will no longer be able to see the letters or the mouth of the inkpot.

I am tired, but Tilla is more so. She has not been able to work much, though she is willing. She rests often. One common explanation comes to my mind. But how could that be, sheltered and chaperoned as Tilla has been?

This morning her nausea was very bad. Her dark hair was damp on the nape of her neck as she leant over the bowl I held for her. I saw how young she is. Not much more than a child, in a strange place, so far from her cushioned life in Rome. She is even more alone now than I was when I first found myself in Italy far from my home and people.

Cosmas was with me, at least. He was all I had. That is why I clung to him so hard, and I wearied him in the end. He became a successful teacher, and his many friends offered dancing girls notorious for their flexibility, and pretty boys. He tired of me. Sometimes he would come back for a while, and I would begin hoping for a child once more.

I cleaned Tilla's mouth. Then, without a word, she stood up, keeping her face tilted away from me, and left the room.

What can I do? Perhaps I can ask Octavius to bring a doctor here?

Old Glauca says to Tilla, Let me look at you properly, I will know what is wrong. But Tilla always refuses. I do not blame her. The old woman makes me shiver, the way she peers out of the corner of her eye. Has she been told to watch us? Spy on us? What evil magic is in the mixtures she is always making of plants and bones and ash and seawater?

About the eleventh day before the kalends of July. About the thirtieth day on Pontia.

This island reminds me of my childhood place. It is like, and yet unlike. We are high up here, and it is like being up on the high camp of my people, the ramparts behind us, the sea far below. But this is a bluer sea, and with almost no tides. Blue like the sky: whereas my sea was more often green or grey, with high waves, white capped, manes of the wild horses. Yet the sound of these waves breaking is an echo of the sea I heard when I was a child. I sat and watched the waves advance and retreat, as the gannets dropped in headfirst, hunting. I loved to gaze at the sea but always feared it. I never went into it, beyond touching my toes to the very edge of the white foam. I never swam in it with the other children.

Inland, away from the sea, were the woods and valleys and their sheltered secrets. Here on Pontia there are not many trees. I long for greenness as never before. And the heat is suffocating, it beats down mercilessly.

It is late afternoon. The rustle of a lizard scurrying back into the undergrowth, the squawk of a startled bird, these sounds startle me.

About the eleventh day before the kalends of July. About the thirty-first day on Pontia.

This is the hottest hour of the afternoon. Tilla is resting. Before I lie down I want to write in these pages. I do indeed wonder if this well-bred young girl has managed, despite all her nursemaids, to find herself a lover: if she is pregnant.

She keeps such distance from me some days. On others she is friendly, as she was this morning, but always with a certain reserve. How can I ask her if it is possible? And when? Just after she wakes up, when she is still drowsy, and perhaps less on her guard? This very afternoon?

***

> *Furthermore, he [the Roman governor of Britain, Agricola] began to educate the sons of the chiefs in the liberal arts, and to give preference to the inborn talents of the Britons as compared with the acquired skills of the Gauls. As a result, where before they loathed the Latin language, now they were eager to speak it eloquently.*
>
> —Tacitus, *Agricola*

Marina's native tongue was not the Latin she wrote in, but ancient British, also called Brythonic or Brittonic; the language that later evolved into Old Welsh, Old Cornish and Old Breton. Apart from a few British names on coins and tombstones, it was a spoken, not a written, language during the centuries of the Roman occupation. To learn to write was to learn to write Latin. What is known of the words and structure of Marina's real language, the language she grew up speaking, has been deduced by scholars from studying those early versions of Welsh, Cornish, and Breton—languages sometimes called Celtic.

Although it has been said that the population in the British Isles at the time of the Roman invasion was "Celtic," some scholars have recently questioned the use of this term. Greek and Roman authors described certain peoples in the ancient world as Celts (*keltoi* in Greek) but all of them lived on the continent of Europe. The inhabitants of the British Isles were never called Celts in ancient times. And archaeologists of the Iron Age agree that no inhabitant of ancient Britain or Ireland would have called him or herself a "Celt" or "Celtic." In fact the people of those places would not have called themselves "Celtic" before the eighteenth century.

The concept of Celtishness has become part of our view of history, something that connects the ancient Irish, Welsh, Scottish, Manx, Cornish, and Breton people. It's a romantic idea for many of us. Yet it is actually a modern construct. Although there were many similarities between the original languages and cultures of the people of the British Isles and those called Celts on the continent, the previous picture of a common Celtic identity has now changed. The understanding of the Iron Age peoples of Britain continues to shift as more discoveries are made.

Marina's manuscript is new evidence in this complex terrain, and the scholars in their different fields will dissect her every word; I leave that to them, but at any rate, she certainly never calls herself or her people Celtic, and therefore nor shall I.

Perhaps when she spoke in her first language, her ancient British tongue, she sounded like a different person from the person we meet on the page; perhaps her thoughts ran in patterns that Latin cannot fully represent.

Even speaking American English as opposed to my native British English gives me a feeling of not being quite myself. If I use ordinary words like "jumper" or "yard" in the way I always have used them, people here do not understand me. To make myself clear, I have had to shift my lexicon. After living here so long, I have forgotten my own language, and I am not sure any more what is British English, and what is American; so I speak and write a hybrid, as these pages witness.

Between Marina's lines, I seem to be trying to leave a trace of myself. I began this book to give the world what she has written, and that is still very important to me, especially as I have not been able to discover how much the archaeologist had completed of his own edition. I also wanted to set her words in their context, and elucidate some of the knotty historical and paleographical issues. And yet, as I transcribe the passages of her manuscript, I find I am leaving her to speak without that sort of annotation. More and more I am inclined—or she leads me—to follow the spirals of my own thoughts and memories. Strange, because I have always kept my own life locked away.

Yet if not now, when? And if not here, sheltered by Marina, in the lee of her words and her story, then where?

About the tenth day before the kalends of July. Thirty-second day on Pontia.

I did ask her yesterday. I went into her room. The door was open for the breeze. I sat on the creaky bed where she lay, awakening, under a coverlet she brought from Rome. It is embroidered with gold and silver and the best purple. Out of place here.

When I told her I wanted to ask her a question, she looked down at her fingers as they played nervously with the coverlet. I asked awkwardly if she had ever been with a man. She looked up at me, still sleepy—then suddenly her mouth twisted, she sat up, and buried her face in her hands. From behind her fingers came a muffled "Yes . . ." and then desperate sobs. I put my arm around her shoulders. She told me to leave her alone.

I did not see her for the rest of the afternoon and evening.

Next morning she came to me as I was eating. She sat down in an old wicker chair with its strips uncoiling. She looked so tired, and yet so very young. With her eyes closed, voice shaking, fingers massaging the ball of amber she holds and rubs it for its piney scent, as her aunt did, she asked me if she could be pregnant. Perhaps, I said. If the man released the seed—she flinched, nodded, eyes squeezed shut.

I asked when was her last monthly flow. She could not remember. Think harder, I snapped at her.

Some say traveling from an inland place to the sea can interrupt it. And she is still a young girl.

The cicadas were loud outside. She sat very still and pale. At last she said she thought it was around the kalends of May.

Soon it will be the kalends of July. Two months, I said, and asked if this is usual for her. No, she replied. Nor are the other things. This tiredness.

And now she is sleeping again.

Who was this man? Though even if there was a man, she may be ill, not pregnant, as I know all too well. It is impossible to discern the body's invisible work. So often, when Cosmas was still with me, I wondered what was happening inside my own belly, hoping there was life, watching for every possible sign.

Is she really sleeping? Or lying awake, afraid?

I wish I had spoken more gently.

Ninth day before the kalends of July. Thirty-third day on Pontia.

Years ago, in Britannia, when the moon changed me from a child into a young woman, the priestess and my mother spoke many prayers for me. They prayed I would have a fine man and a full womb. We made the vows to the powers and spirits of that place according to our ancient customs. Yet I am barren, and sometimes I cannot bear the bitterness of it, of being a woman, yet less than a woman.

Thirty-fourth day on Pontia. Eighth day before the kalends of July.

Neither Tilla nor I have spoken again about pregnancy. Surely in a day or two her body will answer the question and prove there is nothing.

Tilla reads. She studied poetry and philosophy sometimes with her aunt. Now she likes finding old books in the dusty library here.

I seek out things to occupy my hands and mind. I even go into the garden and help Glauca weed the vegetable plot, and harvest the late beans. We try to keep the basil and parsley and thyme from dying of thirst. To support tall, drooping plants, we tie them to sticks of dried broom.

About the thirty-seventh day on Pontia. Around the fifth day before the kalends of July.

Glauca came in when Tilla was ill again. She seems truly concerned about the girl. Or perhaps she is just a curious busybody. Tilla wanted to send her away. But I said, Enough of this. You need help now.

Give her something to make her better, I said to Glauca.

The old woman laughed and said, That depends on what is wrong with her, which I can guess. And on what you mean by making her better.

Glauca stepped forward to where Tilla was lying and touched Tilla's brow. She took her hand, and looked into her eyes. Suddenly I thought, Perhaps she is trustworthy after all.

She asked, Something to help with the sickness, young lady? Or something to make you all better, to bring on the bleeding?

I knew what Glauca meant. I wondered if Tilla would understand, but she did. She sat up straight and said, Something gentle, Glauca, something that you are sure will not do any harm. Something for the sickness only.

Glauca said she would make a poultice of dried dates and pomegranate peel for her stomach, and an infusion of purslane for her to drink.

After Glauca shuffled away I sat beside Tilla, hoping that the old woman has true knowledge of herbs. Hoping she will do as Tilla asks and give her something gentle. But why did Tilla ask this? Why is she so sure she wants medicine that will not harm a pregnancy? I could not ask her, for she closed her eyes as if to sleep, and I left her resting.

The day before the kalends of July.

Tomorrow is the kalends of July, Octavius tells us. It is also the festival of Juno in Rome.

Juno is for married women, said Tilla. She has nothing to do with me.

The treatments Glauca has been giving her help only a little with the sickness.

This must be about the fortieth day that we have been on the island. I have lost count of how long. I do not think it matters any more. We do not know when we will be released. Or if we ever will.

Some days before the nones of July.

The kalends of July have come and gone. Tilla let Glauca examine her today, at last. She asked me to stay in the room. Glauca told Tilla to remove even her breast-band.

She said, Look at these full breasts, these big blue veins. The vomiting, the tiredness, the lack of monthly blood, there is no question: you are pregnant. But I can help you, I can relieve you of the burden.

Tilla sent her away.

All those years I offered sacrifices to Juno, made vows, worshipped Isis, drank potions, hoped so fiercely for this thing that has somehow befallen even Tilla, a young, unmarried girl. This thing that happens to every other woman under the sun, it seems. As long as Cosmas came to my bed, I kept on hoping. Then he left and I could not even hope any more. I sought to draw him back to me, with the help of a woman skilled in magic arts and the secrets of Venus. But Venus did not hear. And even she who is called Great Saviour, Mother of All, Isis herself, even she abandoned me.

. . . Callirhoe, on the other hand, planned to destroy the child, arguing with herself, "Am I to allow a descendant of Hermocrates to be born a slave? Shall I produce a child whose father no one knows? Perhaps some malicious person will say, 'Callirhoe became pregnant among pirates.' It is enough for me alone to suffer. There is no advantage for you, my child, in entering a life of misery. . . ."
. . . Then again she changed her mind, and pity for the unborn child came over her. "Are you planning to kill your child?" she said. "You wicked woman, you are mad and thinking like a Medea. . . ."
—Chariton, *Callirhoe*

Lineage, in the ancient world, was all-important. Not to know who one's father was, to be unable to name him and his father before him, made one almost a non-person; it was a deep disgrace. And to know your father's name did not help your standing if that name meant nothing in the community where you lived.

Callirhoe, the heroine of a wildly romantic Greek novel that Tilla herself may have known, was the daughter of Hermocrates, ruler of Syracuse, and thus nobly born; but she was kidnapped, taken far from her land and from the husband she loved, and sold into slavery by pirates. When she learned she had become pregnant while still with her husband, she felt no personal shame; she was lawfully married. But she feared for what the child would suffer, born into exile and slavery.

Tilla was a young girl of good Roman family. If she had still been in Rome when her pregnancy was discovered, her position there would have been deeply shameful. And even though she was now an exile, this irregular pregnancy added a much more profound disgrace, especially since, unlike Callirhoe, she had never been a bride.

Two thousand years later, in my own world, it was little different. I know something about the shame, and the fear of shame. I know about the anxious waiting, and the denial, the pushing away of such a possibility. Finally, the inevitable tightness of clothes, the swelling of the belly, and the impossibility of ignoring what was happening any longer, or of hiding it. Once the truth was visible in a girl's blossoming body, everyone could see what she had done; then came the humiliation. To be sent away was almost a relief, after the suspicious looks and scandalised murmurs. Or at least I found it so.

I have surprised myself, revealing this. That it happened to me. This is something I have never told anyone or written down before.

When I came back from Italy all those years ago, it was still summer, and my course of study, the master's meant to lead to a doctorate, had not started up again. Researching the history of Ponza almost every day, in my self-imposed distraction project, I fiercely smothered my emotions; and I ignored my body as well, implicated with those emotions as it was in every fibre. So it was only gradually that I noticed I was feeling a little strange all the time, and my period was late.

At first I refused to worry, but then I could no longer keep anxiety at bay; it invaded me. That was a long lonely time of struggle, and my mother began to see there was something wrong. There were no do-it-yourself tests then. I told her I did not feel well. Perhaps it was a lingering effect of the bout of food poisoning I'd had in Italy, I said. And so I made an appointment with the doctor, where of course the truth could no longer be denied. He told me I was three months into pregnancy. And I had to go home and face my mother.

There were rigid standards then for what was respectable. I was not married, or even engaged; I had "fallen pregnant"—these were the phrases used, you had "fallen pregnant," or "got yourself pregnant," as if there were no one else involved. I was expecting a baby out of wedlock. I was a shameful blot on society.

My mother did not let me forget this. For the first few months of the pregnancy, until it began to show, I lived under her scorn and disapproval. I was at home all the time because I had to withdraw from my studies, and so I felt this every moment of every day, although after the first dreadful conversation we never spoke of what had happened. She kept an eye on my physical condition, she made sure I ate and stayed healthy, but she would not say a word about my emotional state, my all-too-evident sorrow. It seemed clear she considered my misery entirely deserved, brought upon myself by my own stupidity. I withdrew, first in self-protection, and then gradually also to guard the life inside me.

Because a strange thing happened as time went on: even as my mind recoiled, my body chose to move carefully, plotted the wellbeing of its new cargo. Without realizing what I was doing, I found myself keeping away from disturbances and noise and crowds, seeking places of safety. For me, there was no truly safe place: I myself was a battlefield, sometimes overwhelmed with searing shame, sometimes strangely protective. Slowly my mind began to accept my body's growing heaviness. And then I started to feel that strange fluttering inside. The unseen passenger was becoming a companion.

A few days before the nones of July.

This morning, as Tilla nibbled a crust, Glauca shuffled by, a filthy rag in her hand. She does not seem to realise that her rag leaves more dirt behind than it picks up. She peered into Tilla's face and said: It is time for the strong herbs. You should not wait.

Tilla got up and went away.

I write in these pages as if doing so will smooth everything.

Glauca offers Tilla the strong herbs but Tilla dismisses her. Is she afraid? She should be. I have seen many a woman die of these herbs and pessaries, sometimes her own doing, sometimes forced by a husband or father to evict her unborn child.

Does Tilla want to be pregnant?

Flavia Domitilla told me to take care of this girl. What would she, what would Flavius Clemens, have done? Would they have made Tilla rid herself of the child, seeking to preserve the family's good name? Would they have found out who fathered the child and forced a marriage? Would they have had her bear the child and then abandon it?

Such questions are futile. She is not in Rome, she is here. She is an exile, in disgrace. The consul is dead. Tilla's future, the possibility of a connection with the eligible son of some worthy family, is all gone.

Here, only the heat, the sea below us, the unending days on this island.

Can I let Tilla play knucklebones with her life? Not that I could stop her doing anything she sets her mind to. I know that to my cost already.

And what is more dangerous? Glauca's strong herbs? Or to carry the baby and give birth?

Already I find myself becoming tender towards the thought of what is growing inside her slim young belly.

I wish my mother, with her skill in helping women, were here with us.

Third day before the nones of July.

Today we went down the long stairs cut in the rock, down to the fish pools, for the festival. There are about six enclosures, some with various types of fish, two with eels of different kinds. Some of the eels are for the table, but a select few have a holy task.

One of those cave rooms has patterns made of shells and chips of coloured stone on the walls and on the curved ceiling. A pillar rising out of the central pool supports a statue: Apollo. He is beautiful, the bright one, the healer, like Belenos of my people. He brings light to this place of darkness under the cliff where land meets sea.

Some of the eels are yellow or silvery, serpentlike. But another kind is large with a heavier head. These are morays, sleek fat things, with skin mottled and flecked, sometimes almost golden. They seem to smile in a mysterious way, as if they know secrets. They hide among the large rocks that have been placed in the pools for them. They pass in and out of their caverns.

Many people had gathered in the cave sanctuary. The garrison commander was there, and the harbourmaster, and the procurator: all with power over Tilla and me. A little daylight came from the cave entrance, from outside, where the boat landing is, and there were torches. Around each pool is a path of wooden planks. The boards are slippery. I kept away from the edge. The priest made an offering at the altar in a niche in the wall and prayed to Apollo. He asked the god to speak through the movements of the eels. One of the fishery men scattered food on the water to make the eels come. Then another took a great net and scooped up three squirming morays and tipped them into a wide, shallow bowl in front of the altar. The augur called on Apollo for vision. He leaned forward to look into the bowl and watch how the morays would swim. Tilla and I were too far away to see. After silent moments, he stood up straight and began to chant, his voice echoing between the cave walls and over the water. This was the message of the god:

There will be good fortune on this island, fair weather and full nets.

Tilla was beside me, watching, listening. Her face an unreadable mystery.

As the musicians played in honour of Apollo I thought about the promised good fortune, wondering if it could touch exiles too. Then a fishery worker walked along the slippery planks in front of me. As he passed, carrying titbits for the eels, his eyes met mine and he smiled in a friendly way. He tipped the food in. The water became a swirling mass of eels, curling under and over each other. As I stared, they seemed like the great birds on my grandfather's shield, legs, necks, wings, all looping and twisting. Or like the knotted magic of the etching on the arm of the druid. His hand lifted high, calling on the powers, his sleeve falling back to reveal the dark design against the skin of his forearm white in the early sun, he chanted as they led me to the boat, as they helped me in, as they pushed the boat out into the water.

Here on this alien island, old memories come back more and more. For so many years, traveling with Cosmas, learning to write, I could not think about my own country. Nor did I want to. We grew close as we traveled in ramshackle boats and rickety carriages. We spoke in a mixture of Latin and Greek and the few words he knew of my language. At first he had seemed so old to me. He had already taken and lost a wife, she who died in the earthquake, still childless. But he won me subtly, and with knowledgeable hands. When he left me, I had to learn to live alone and work alone. If my home and my people came to mind, I banished them from my thoughts. All this time my life has been uncoiling outward, away from the place where I was born. Now, my memory loops back there.

Day before the nones of July.

Today Tilla came with a dish of food to where I was sitting. I had eaten the midday meal without her. I had not seen her all morning.

She said nothing for a while: just ate her eggs and bread. I found myself gazing at her. She looked back at me, strangely calm.

Then she said:

I am an exile and a prisoner. I have lost my family for a second time. I have no honour or name left to preserve. Marina, do you remember how my aunt Flavia Domitilla's baby drank at her breast? How he followed her with his eyes around the room, and cried when she went away? I do not want Glauca's strong medicine. If a child is growing inside me, then that is one thing I have not lost. It is my own.

This was the first time she had talked so openly to me.

But then I said, What happened? Who is the father?

She stood up quickly and went away, saying only, Do not ask.

I am writing in the heat of the afternoon, in the shade of a high wall. Even here it is stifling. Flies buzz around me, the air hangs heavy. I will go and rest.

If space permits, it is a good idea to place rocks from the seashore, covered with clumps of seaweed, in different parts of the fish pond, and to create as artfully as one can the appearance of the sea; so that although they are prisoners, the fish may feel their captivity as little as possible.

—Columella, *On Agriculture*

In my American life there are pieces of rock and strands of seaweed that give me the impression of being at home. Some of them I have put in the pool myself. Nevertheless, England has always pulled me back, with a strong, a steady undertow. I feel it more and more as the years pass.

Whenever I visit England, I realise that after so many years in America I have forgotten much of my own language, and what I do remember is often not the way people speak now. Some words—wheelie-bin, whinge—are quite new to me, and others seem to have changed meaning. But then a blackbird sings, or a thrush; or some drizzly day I walk between the worn tombstones in a country churchyard, push open the creaking church door, and step into the smell of wax and musty hassocks. I feel at home in England then; but it does not last. As Milan Kundera has said about emigration, worse than the pain of nostalgia is the pain of estrangement on returning to the native land after a long absence.

I belong neither here nor there.

Books have become my country. I still love libraries as I did in my earliest childhood. I often go into the university library to inhale its particular seductive smell, and explore the secrets of its dark stacks. It is where I feel at home.

That is not enough, however; I need to possess books, see them peopling the bookshelves in my rooms, from floor to ceiling. They are part of whatever it is that holds me here. I brought no books with me when I fled from England; I was traveling light. Over the years I have, almost without meaning to, accumulated titles that evoke home. If I were to go back to England, would I take with me P.G. Wodehouse, Dickens, Ivy Compton-Burnett? What of gloomy Philip Larkin, acerbic yet funny Barbara Pym?

My books reflect my divided life, so I also have American writers like Henry Roth and Anne Tyler, Emerson and James. Then there are the biographies and memoirs. The shapes of people's lives fascinate me, their struggles and their paths of self-discovery. Perhaps even more delightful are the books about eccentric people—the more eccentric, the better, in a book at least. I suspect I like people more on the page than in reality.

Suppose I were to sell this house, what would the new owners do with my garden? They would probably rip out the sweet autumn clematis when it looks grey and nondescript; not knowing where all the bulbs are buried, they might disturb my daffodils, dig up my snowdrops or grape hyacinths.

When I came to America, I wanted the challenge of being in an unfamiliar place, and of a new and difficult kind of work. And that is what I had, first as a real estate agent, trying to find the perfect home for other people while not knowing where my own home really was, and then as the high school history teacher I eventually became.

In the summers I have been able to pursue my passion for history, paleography and codicology. I audited courses, went to conferences, took every opportunity I could to learn, but in little pieces, whenever I could find some time. I have even published a few specialist papers—none of them taken seriously in academia, of course.

At first I did not return to England at all. Then I began going back as opportunities arose, but I avoided the places I had loved before. I could not bear to see the green curves of my Mendip Hills.

After everything that had happened between us, my mother and I were distant. We conducted a stiff, irregular correspondence when I was in the States. On my earlier trips back to England, I did not even tell her I was in the country. Then I visited her once or twice; I knew my distance was hurting her. I was her only child, after all, and I had no father. He was an American GI who had married her and then abandoned her before I was born. Also I began to miss her strong presence in my life. The power of the past began to fade, and we edged a little closer, tentatively. But my sojourns in England have always been awkward; not true homecomings.

I've built a semblance of a home here in the States. I live in the outer suburbs of a small city. There are places where I go for calm and solace; a certain lake edged with dark trees, a hill with a view of forested slopes stretching into the distance. I have several friends, although I suppose it's true I have no intimate friend in whom I could confide if I needed to. And I must admit to a certain loneliness because my few close relationships with men foundered. I have always blamed the men, or the circumstances, but this new strange self-decipherment on which I seem to have embarked compels me to admit that some of the responsibility was mine. It seems I cannot help but bristle if someone threatens my barricades.

A successful single woman, that's me.

When I heard of the archaeologist's death a month or so ago, I intended to make plans for a long visit to England. First I had to try and discover where he kept the original codex, and see it again for myself; then I needed to think about the direction of my own life. I might have looked into the possibility of one day returning permanently, or at least of tackling some of my unfinished business.

But my body has let me down with its strange, niggling complaints; and now I am waiting for the diagnosis.

About ten days before the kalends of August. Festival of
Neptunalia.

When my mother tried to teach me a new weave or basket pattern, I longed instead to be running in the wind or down on the shingle watching the sea. I did not listen to what she was saying. If only I could hear her voice now, saying any word at all. The last time I saw her, she was crying, with a strange distorted face. I lay strapped to the couch in those heavy robes. I was drowsy. I did not understand why she and my father were sad. As they were led away from me, my mother looked back with an expression of terrible pain.

All I have of her now is the cloth she wove, and the mirror wrapped in it. Today I unfolded the cloth, with the patterns her fingers made, the crisscrossing colours of the sea.

What are you weaving, mother? I asked.

Something for you, to keep you warm, she said.

But the cloth is too small for that. She was never able to finish the work.

Today I looked at the mirror of my mother and her mother and her mother's mother before her. I traced with my finger the curves in the back of it, the designs like basketwork, like birds, like wings.

Will I die here? Will these things stay on this island, so far from the place where they belong?

Two days before the kalends of August.

The heat is heavy and oppressive. Today Tilla said, Let us swim.

I reminded her that Glauca says it is dangerous for a pregnant woman. Tilla said she can bear the heat no longer.

I will swim gently, she said. My aunt swam at Baiae even when her baby was near being born.

She led the way down the steep stairs in the rock, down the side of the cliff to the sea below. I watched her climbing down in front of me, her hair lifted off her neck, the dark curls thrust into a hairnet of gold wire. Her neck is as brown as a farmer's now.

We reached a place where there is a flat rock and the water lapped against it, waist-deep. Tilla slid into it and so did I. I stood beside her and we relished the coolness of the water over our feet, legs, and thighs. It felt so delicious around our hips.

But then Tilla began to swim away from the rock, slowly and carefully, on her side. She wanted me to join her. And so she found out that I do not know how to swim.

She has begun teaching me. She supports my body in the water, and she says, Feel how not only I hold you, but the water holds you. It is strong.

I know already that the sea is strong.

She showed me how to move my arms and legs. We will try every day, she says, until I am ready for her to release me into the water, ready to swim alone.

She teaches me with surprising gentleness and does not mock me.

About three days before the ides of August.

The time of harvesting crops is ending. Here the people make use of every little patch they can carve out of this rocky land. The small fields of grain have been cut, and everyone is waiting for the stalks to finish drying so the straw can be gathered.

I have not written for some time. Now Tilla's sickness is for the most part gone and so is the deep fatigue, although the heat of the day tires her. In the very early morning, or in the evening cool, she walks along the paths, and climbs up and down from terrace to terrace. I walk with her sometimes.

We have continued the swimming lessons. She brought a gourd down to the water from Glauca's store, and showed me how it floats. I held it and she put her hands under my belly as usual to support me. I kicked my legs and swam a little. Then she took her arms away, but the gourd floated, and I was not afraid but floated behind it, holding on to it and kicking. I swam a few strokes, and we laughed together triumphantly.

When Tilla sits and rests for a while, she sews or spins wool. Sometimes she reads.

Today she asked me about the books in my country. My people have no writings, I told her.

How do they remember their past? she asked.

I told her how learning is kept in the minds of our poets and priests. How they give it to their chosen pupils, make them recite and repeat over and over again, for many years, until they have it all by heart. They know the tales of the ancestors and the ways to reach the place where the ancestors have gone. They know the pathways of the stars, the pattern of the future, and the shape of time.

But you can write, she said.

Yes, I told her, but writing was a new thing when I learned it. Some of the older people say it weakens the memory to write things down instead of remembering them.

I am forgetting even my own life. Indeed, at first I wanted to forget. But now I see there are parts I would like to remember. Fragments come into my mind and then are gone. I will try and catch them, so they do not slip away like eels, or like these lizards that disappear in a flicker.

I offered to give Tilla some more writing lessons to help pass the time, and as a recompense for her teaching me to swim. She said she would like that.

The Druid Broccomagus spoke about the dangers of writing. There was a night in the house of feasts. Torcs glinted in the firelight around the muscled throats of our princes, my father among them. The lamps fell here and there on the many colours of fine cloaks. The poet had finished a new song and there was shouted praise, and drinking of his health.

Then Broccomagus stood up to speak and the voices quieted. He was admired and feared. He had grown up among my people and studied the ancient learning. He had gone to the holy grove on the island of Mona. When the Romans destroyed it, he escaped, some said in the form of a gull or a whale, and he came back to his native place. He refused to set foot in the new town the Romans were building a morning's ride away. He would only enter houses that were round, without corners, as we had always built them. He thought our young warriors, forbidden to carry weapons, were growing soft with baths and warm floors. He ignored the Roman ban on druidry, and continued sacrifices and soothsayings in the dark places in the woods. That night he spoke with bitterness, saying something like this:

You think by giving your children these pens and tablets, you are giving them a gift? No indeed, it is not so. You are taking something precious away. Their minds will be full of Roman things. Who will remember the stories of our people? Who will submit to the long learning, the salting away of knowledge in the mind and heart? Who will understand trees, and rivers, and seasons? Who will know how to call on the ancient powers of the hills and forests?

There was a silence as he paused. He stood tall and proud, his hair falling iron-grey down his back. A cloak of all colours draped his shoulders, and his massive torc glinted in the candlelight. His hair was shaved away at the front in the old style of the druids. He usually hid this baldness under a hood. Now his huge brow extended nakedly right to the top of his head. It shone in a way that was frightening to see.

I glanced at my father. These words were an insult to him, he who had engaged a tutor to teach my brother and me to write. Fortunately the tutor himself, Cosmas, was not there. Broccomagus spoke again and his voice was like a sword.

It is death to the old ways! It is death to our people! We will lose the protection of the ancestors for ever! The three mothers will not watch over us, the hooded ones will lock themselves in their deep places in the hills, the stag-headed lord of the woods will not hear our prayers: because we shall have forgotten the old ways of our people.

And he strode out into the darkness.

My father and the other older men said all over again what they had said many times before: What else can we do? These Romans have been here a whole generation now. We pay them the tribute and they take away our young men. We must use them to our advantage. We must beat them at their own games of writing and accounting, and let our girls marry them. We must take our power back by stealth, wherever we can.

Despite what the men said, the words of Broccomagus still hung in the air. Speech in his mouth had terrible power. Soon I felt that power against me.

A few days before the kalends of September.

I am thirsty. The ration of water from the cisterns is not enough, the aqueduct does not bring more unless there has been rain. The salt sea is so huge, so wide, so much a distance keeping us from Rome, and yet it cannot quench the thirst.

I love to swim in it with Tilla, though. It is a cool delight.

Glauca and Octavius say the drought is worse this year than usual.

There is talk that the grapes may ripen early because of the heat.

Soon before the ides of September.

The sea mists in the morning here are soft and with a tang of salt. After the feast of Vulcan, Glauca said it was time for the third sowing. We planted radishes, turnips and alexanders, working in the morning coolness. I think of my own country. There was a salt smell there, but different, because of more trees, ferns, different plants. What was it like? I strain my memory to breathe it again but I cannot catch it.

The inside of our house, built against the flank of the great grassy hill, had walls of branches, twisted and interwoven like the sides of a basket. The supporting limbs, made from slim trunks of young trees, reached up to a point in the roof. The smoke coiled up there in the dark, where the spiteful house imps lived. In the winter, the pigs jostled us for space.

To a Roman like Tilla, that house would not be worthy of the name, twigbuilt as it was, thatched with straw, and with no window openings, let alone glass panes. But I belonged there.

After all these years of trying to forget, now the sorrow of exile from my land comes over me. I feel a longing to be where I know the shape of the hills, and the song of the birds is familiar.

Tilla and I have been exiled by Domitianus. But I was in exile already, ever since that day I was cast off in the boat. Only now do I fully taste its bitterness.

I am like a sapling wrenched from its piece of earth. A limpet from its rock.

How could I ever go back to my own place? Just to leave this island, I must step into a boat again and sail back to the mainland. Then there is the long long road though Italia and Gallia, and after that the terrible ocean. And even if I should reach the shore of my country, I cannot set foot there. Broccomagus laid binding words on me, the most terrible words, a spell against returning.

Mid-September.

We help Glauca with the tasks of the season. Tilla and Chloë and I dry figs on frames raised off the ground, covering them at sunset with straw against the dew. Then we seal them in large vessels with the soft woolliness of fennel leaves, picked and dried last year, around them. We dry apples and pears in the sun too, and, in the shade, herbs, to be preserved in salt and vinegar.

Glauca says all these things will be precious to us in the winter. We are also preparing for the grape harvest, cleaning vessels for wine and vinegar, and scouring them with seawater.

Glauca's husband and the household boys set snares for the countless migrating birds that fill the skies and land on the island during their journey.

Sometimes Tilla forgets I am a foreign barbarian and we talk almost like friends.

Today, as we rested during the afternoon heat, she lay on a couch Glauca has tried to improve with an old piece of brocade. The fabric's purples and greens are faded, but still rich even in the shadows. On the small table beside Tilla was a bowl of fresh figs, some of the few Glauca allows us to eat in their juicy prime. The shutters were closed against the heat, still strong although the summer is coming towards an end. There are suddenly more and more flies everywhere, even indoors, however tightly we close everything. The people say this means the grapes will soon be ready.

Tilla read part of a book by Lucretius to me today, and we talked about it until we began to understand it.

Lucretius says objects continually throw off flimsy films, like cast-off skins. The air is filled with these images. We do not see objects themselves, he says, but the images cast off from them. These images cannot pass through wood or stone, so we do not see the image of a table on the other side of the wall. But the images can travel right through glass.

When an image comes up against a polished surface like the metal of my mother's mirror, it is not blocked, nor does it pass through. It is caught and reflected. So I see the image of my face in the mirror, but dimly, because the fragile film is damaged from being bounced against the mirror and tossed back in reverse.

Objects throw off other images, says Lucretius, even more fragile than the ones our eyes see: the images that enter our minds. They are always flying through the air. Sometimes they stick together—so the centaur, for example, comes from the combined images of horse and man.

These images are invisible. But all around us. We can prepare the mind to receive them. We can think of a certain thing, and the mind becomes ready to receive the image of that object. Then we can catch the image, even in our sleep.

So in my far-off land, the beach and cliffs and village are all casting off images of themselves. If these skins are being shed all the time, could one or two survive the long journey over winds and waves, and reach me here? Could an image of my mother or my father arrive at this island, like a bedraggled bird, homing into my mind at last?

It has never happened, not even in my sleep. Perhaps because for so long I tried not to think of those things. I wanted to forget the last time I saw my mother's face, and what happened to my horse, and the words of Broccomagus when the boat with no oars was pushed out into the sea.

Yet I do want to remember what I loved. The cliff. The cove. The haze on the hills in the morning. The dark skeins of seaweed on the waves. And the people, my mother and father, my brother and little sister. If I think of them, will my mind grow ready to catch their invisible images?

Tilla says Lucretius cannot be right. She thinks very often of Flavia Domitilla. Yet Flavia Domitilla's image never comes to her when she is awake or asleep, although she longs for it. At this I said again that she should write a letter telling Flavia Domitilla everything. And she agreed at last.

The most momentous development in the history of the book until the development of printing was the replacement of the roll by the codex . . .

—Colin H. Roberts and
T.C. Skeat, *The Birth of the Codex*

Bring the cloak that I left at Troas with Carpas when you come, and the books, and especially the parchments.
                    —*The Bible*, 2 Timothy 4:13

Let me sing the praises of the codex book, so uniquely perfect for the keeping of histories, tales, and memories. The oral epic, always told slightly differently according to the time and place of the telling, and always holding the audience in the moment, inhabits the eternal now. The ancient scroll is awkward; you read it by rolling up the part you have finished in one hand, where it is hidden, and what you have not yet read is rolled up in the other hand, equally inaccessible. When you reach the end of the book-roll, neither you nor the next reader can start at the beginning again until the whole text has been unrolled and rolled up in the right direction once more. The computer only allows you to see one "page" at a time, and they are not real pages, there is no physical place to turn to and find what was written before or what comes after; so each segment feels fragmented, and the shape and pattern of a whole text is hard to see.

The birth of the codex, the evolution from the scroll to codex book, is one of the mysteries of the ancient world. In the first century AD, codex books were rare, especially for literary works; by the end of the fourth, they were more common than scrolls. But we have only had tantalizing glimpses of how this happened.

It seems that doctors, architects and other artisans were the first to use pieces of leather or parchment bound together as notebooks. These probably emerged in Rome in the latter part of the first century; small fragments of such notebooks have survived. Also in Rome towards the end of the first century, the poet Martial, in his epigrams on Saturnalia gift ideas, suggests the works of famous authors like Virgil, Cicero, and Ovid in an unusual format: on parchment pages instead of a scroll. You could have the novelty of Homer *pugillaribus membraneis*, "in parchment notebooks." *Pugillares* (from *pugnus*, hand or fist) means a hand-size group of tablets or other writing materials; a notebook. *Membraneis* means made of skin, membrane, parchment. This new kind of book held much more material than a roll. "Vast Livy, compressed in the thinnest of skins," says Martial. Sheet upon sheet like filo pastry; a book like baklava. Compared to the scroll, it was lightweight, compact, and easy to travel with. However, from the archaeological record, this kind of book does not seem to have caught on right away, except among the Christians.

When Paul, or someone writing in his name after he died, sent a letter in Greek to Timothy about the things he left at Troas, and ended by telling Timothy to bring the books, "especially the parchments," he used a Latin noun (in Greek form), *membranas*, which means "skins" or "pieces of leather." At some point this word by itself apparently came to mean a parchment notebook; perhaps it already did so by the time the Second Letter to Timothy was written. Surviving pieces of books show that Christians embraced the codex form much more quickly than others did. As Christianity spread, so did the use of the codex made from parchment and also from papyrus, until by the fourth century it was the standard type of book for almost everyone.

At the end of the first century, when Marina was writing, the codex was just beginning to emerge as a new kind of book, a new technology. (Her own notebook is parchment, and she usually calls it simply *membranae*, "the parchments." But when she speaks of notebooks in a general sense, as opposed to scrolls, she says *pugillares*.) No one could have imagined then that the codex would become the standard format, just as, when the earliest paperbacks appeared, or the first colossal computers, we could not imagine the role they have now in everyday life.

I recognize the usefulness of the computer, although I have chosen not to have one of my own. I am afraid to become too dependent on it, and afraid that I might thus contribute, in however small a way, to the demise of the book.

The codex book fits so well the experience of living; it holds the past, present and future all together. The past is simple to revisit: you can riffle back the leaves, or even keep a bookmark or a finger in a place you want to find again. The present is the page you are reading now. The future is easily stepped into, you can flip forward and see what is to come, and even compare it with the present and the past. A book has a physical shape we can see and touch and understand; it's held together by the spine, the covers, the stitching; it's a cradle, a vessel, a body.

And what of a blank book, as this one was before I began? It is like a life unlived. As I write in it, its past grows, and it has its present moment, this page I am on now. The future pages constitute a terra incognita. I know Marina's text, of course, but not at what places it will make room for my own antiphons; nor what the words of those will be.

One can always turn over a new leaf, which as a child I imagined meant going out into the woods and turning over leaf after leaf on the ground until you discovered a new one. Then I learned that a leaf was a page, and you could turn over a new leaf when you had blotted your copybook. Although in life it is not always so simple.

My own future is now a dark and unknown place indeed; *here be dragons*. The doctors have made their diagnosis, their prognosis, and it is hard to come to terms with what they are telling me. But I have understood there is even more urgency than before about finishing this work.

Halloween has come and gone, with its ghosts and skulls. I prefer All Hallows Day itself, the day of all saints known and unknown. I like to think of them rejoicing together in some invisible dimension, regardless of the different epochs and countries they lived in and languages they used to speak. If only I could really believe it.

Lying here on the sofa, the book leaning against my knees on this cloudy November day with the last coppery leaves blowing down, I begin to understand that this notebook, while containing Marina's story, is also the vessel for my journey now.

Between the ides of September and the kalends of October.

The grapes are ripe. Glauca's husband Philemon has harvested the few vines on the villa property, and goes every day to help in other vineyards. We had a special feast to celebrate the vintage, with the best meats, cheeses, and fish we could afford. Just those of us who live and work here, and a few others, like the wife of Octavius and relatives of Glauca and Philemon.

Tilla's belly is no longer flat but rounded, beginning to grow.

The moon is waning and the days are clear, so Glauca has been picking certain of the grapes to dry as raisins.

I am bleeding, it is my time of the moon. Glauca does not want me in the garden. It affects the plants, she says. Only when there are too many slugs should a woman walk in the garden in this condition. She must still take care not to touch the plants, but the slugs will fall off and die.

Before I was given my woman's name I was called "little bird" or "minnow" or "mouse." When the bleeding began, my mother told me: We will have the ceremony at the next full moon. And after that we will find the name that is destined for you. You are a woman now—and she took me in her arms with tender excitement.

In the temple there was a carving of the Three Mothers with babies on their laps.

Beside them, a huge round rock rose up from the ground, smooth on top from all the hands and offerings of women before me. The stone had been in that place always, sacred to the Mothers, before the walls were built to enclose it, before the carving was set up nearby.

The priestess, Alauna, told me to take off my childhood brace-let and place it on the rock. She made me kneel on the ground in front of the rock, with my arms around it. My hands pressed into it on either side, fingers spread, palms listening to the stone. She chanted a song to the Mothers, asking that my births be easy and my babies strong, that my breasts give milk to many sons and daughters.

But I know now that the Mothers have punished me.

Then my mother stepped forward with the mirror, and said three blessings:

May your face in this mirror always be glad.

May your life as a woman be bright with joy.

May your children live to cherish you in your old age, and may your first daughter receive the mirror from you as you receive it now from me.

I carried the mirror as we came out of the shrine into the dusk.

My father, brother, and Broccomagus were waiting, and my father spoke the customary words to me. Broccomagus laid his iron fingers on my head. A fat moon rose in the wintry sky.

I only lived among my people as a woman for a short while. Too quickly came the disappearance of the fish, the hungry time, and the casting off of the boat.

A little before the ides of October.

Everyone is still busy with the harvest and the celebration of new wine.

This morning we were walking on a veranda high above the sea. Suddenly Tilla stopped and held her just-curving belly with an expression of astonishment.

She said, It moved! Inside me, it moved. And her face filled with delight.

I asked how the movement felt.

Like a moth in your closed hand, she said.

This girl so much younger than me already knows how it feels to have a child moving inside her.

The ides of October.

Today Tilla told me she is afraid to give birth to a child she cannot love.

She said, I do almost love it already. But I have dreams that it will be born a monster—a child with a snake's body, or a child's body but a dog's head.

Glauca has frightened her with stories about how seeing this animal or that bird can affect the shape of the child in the womb. My people had such stories too. I remember the women talking when I was a girl. My mother used to say they were mostly nonsense—though it was true, she said, that if a hare ran across the path of a pregnant woman, the baby would have a split lip. My mother did not like the old women to frighten the younger ones. A fearless woman has an easy birth, she used to say.

Towards the end of October.

Now they are harvesting the olives and beginning to press them for oil. There are not many olive trees on this rocky, windswept terrain. Every single fruit is precious.

There is a coolness in the air, especially in the mornings and evenings. In Rome, in summertime, the wealthy host sends for ice from the tops of mountains. He has it brought back fast before it melts, and serves it, flavoured and coloured, as a chilly delicacy, eaten on a silver spoon. Here this summer the days were so hot and we were so parched. How we would have relished a spoonful of ice slipping between our dry lips. But those days are gone and soon we will be longing for warmth.

Glauca has traded some vegetables from her garden for many bags of wool. It is to be woven into cloth during the winter. Tilla gave Glauca one of her rings as payment for some of the wool, and for herbs to dye it. We decided to weave a blanket for the baby. This led us to talk of the swaddling bands that Romans use to wrap infants tightly, believing this is how they grow straight and finely shaped. In my country we do not wrap our babies like that, and they grow well just the same. I told Tilla this and she laughed. She said her aunt used to keep unwrapping the baby to admire his little legs and feet and let him kick. The nurse complained, but Flavia Domitilla would reply, I did this to all of them, and look how fine and tall they are.

Today Glauca had the boys set up a two-person loom. Chloë helped us string up the warp threads. Tilla and I will work on the blanket together.

Next day.

As we sit at our weaving, Tilla sometimes asks me about my life when I was a girl.

I try to answer her. But it is hard to speak in Latin about things I only knew in my own tongue, about life so long ago, so far away. It is all distant to me now.

Say something in your language, she asked. There came to my mind part of a lullaby my mother used to sing. I sang a little of it. I could only remember a few of the words. It was about a bird in a tree, I told her. That song has almost vanished from my memory. But other words from my childhood have been coming back to me and I whisper them to myself.

Today Tilla asked, Did you mind leaving? Did you love your husband so much it was easy to go with him and leave your family, your home?

She wants to hear a romance, a fable.

All I have ever said is that Cosmas brought me with him from Britannia. I have not wanted to speak about the boat without oars. So now I told Tilla that the idea of leaving home did not seem strange. There was an old tradition that girls and boys were sometimes sent to live with other families for a while. Although this was not much practised any more, I knew people it had happened to.

Tilla said, Like me, adopted by my aunt and uncle.

Something like that, I said. And then I was silent.

She knows I am keeping so much locked away. For the first time, I think about telling everything, telling it to her.

A few days before Hilaria.

Some days ago, it was the birthday of the emperor. We were afraid that the guards would come and force us to perform sacrifices for him. But they did not.

The sea is often grey now as the weather changes.

Sometimes I give Tilla a writing lesson. She has become skilful and her writing has a swift gracefulness.

I have been hoping Tilla will ask me again about my own country. For so many years I have not spoken of it. Now, with Tilla, I like to remember things. But not everything. Today she asked if we hated the Romans.

I said we had been living under Rome since my father was born. So it was not new, even for my parents. My grandmother told me of the time when the Romans came, when she was carrying my father in her belly. She with all the people and their animals went up to our hilltop sanctuary, high above the sea, behind the palisades and the earthworks. But our warriors with their swords and slingshots could not defend the fortress against the Roman catapults and siege machines. In the terrible battle, her own husband died. He never saw his child. Prisoners and hostages were taken and she was fortunate to be unharmed.

After that, she wanted peace at all costs and taught my father to want the same. He grew up accustomed to the Roman soldiers marching, building, enforcing their laws and taxes. He grew up knowing he could never carry weapons except to hunt, or to fight for the Romans. The burden of the conquerors was heavy. There was much bitterness among the people. There always were some rebels. In my childhood Broccomagus encouraged this. He held forbidden gatherings at night in the woods, and groomed young men to provoke the Romans. The Romans usually caught and killed them.

Tilla has seen triumphal processions with my people paraded in chains. Now she looked at me, and I saw her understanding that my people were brave. We are ashamed of our defeat.

I made her laugh telling of my father, who one chilly day took me with him on a long ride in a wagon to visit the new town Durnovaria. This town was near the fortress of another people, once our enemy. In the face of Roman invasion they had become our allies. There were many wooden buildings, and one basilica of stone where all the leaders of our two peoples could gather.

We went inside. He told me to take off my shoes and stand in my bare feet.

Feel that, he whispered. Feel the floor—warm! And the air—warm!

It was so cold in my land in winter, especially when the wind howled in off the sea. Even when you wore layers of wool over wool, the dampness chilled to the bone.

In our houses we had nothing like heated floors or hot baths. Just little bowls of water warmed over the fire. Taking off our clothes to wash was a rare thing. Suddenly, now, I imagine, for the briefest moment, the smell of wet wool drying in front of the hearth.

End of the festival of Hilaria.

The six days of the festival of Hilaria are over. Last night was the procession down to the sea with torches to celebrate the joy of Isis, Isis Pelagia, queen of the waves, who found her lost beloved.

As I watched the procession I prayed to the lady Isis Pelagia, powerful goddess on this rock in the midst of water. I asked the eternal mother for her protection over me, and over Tilla and her unborn baby. I asked her to forgive my anger that she had not cured my barrenness. Perhaps that was a gift after all. What might have happened to a child when I was sent to this sea-surrounded island?

The very name Pontia means "of the deep sea." This is an island born of the sea, like Venus herself.

Tilla said, Why is your name Marina, a name of the sea?

I told her the name was given to me when I went to seek it, according to the tradition of my people. But the sound is different, the way we say it, I told her, and I spoke my name as my people did. She repeated it, not exactly, but close enough. It was strange to hear. I have not heard that in anyone's mouth for so long.

The evening I went out to find my name was windy and cold.
It was winter, soon after the womanhood ceremony, and about
two months before the spring festival.

Despite the weather, the signs were good. An auspicious day. As
is our custom, I was alone with an older woman, my father's sister, Lavinia. She was respected for her knowledge of the signs of
birds and clouds and the sea. We were to stay outside from sunset to sunset, a whole night and a day, to receive the name.

Lavinia and I set up our hide tent and made a fire. She had chosen the traditional place on the clifftop, the turf walls behind us,
the wide expanse of the sea before. The sea was rough, the whole
day had been stormy and the men could not go out fishing. We
made a circle of stones around our little fire, against the wind.
Lavinia threw herbs on the fire to make the flames holy and she
said prayers for wisdom. I asked why we needed to be in the path
of the wind, not in a sheltered place. She said the wind might
blow the name into our minds. Or it might speed our sleeping
travels. In the night, she or I or both of us would fly out in our
spirits and discover my name. We drank the infusion of dream-
ing herbs, and lay down in our furs and blankets. The darkness
pressed on us all around with its unseen creatures. I was afraid
of the night journey and could not fall asleep for a long time.

In the morning, I knew I had slept little, but I had no memory of
anything happening in the night. I found Lavinia pacing to keep
warm. She stood still and looked at me gravely.

She said, I did not dream a name for you. I saw a boat tied up at
low tide, a boat that could not sail. It means we must wait. We
have time, until the sun goes down again.

The morning passed. It grew a little warmer as the sun, often
hidden by clouds, moved across the sky. We rested and watched
the seabirds flying, sometimes buffeted by the wind. We spoke
of many things. Lavinia told me some of the secrets of women.

Sometimes we stood and stretched and walked a little.

Towards the end of the afternoon, I went across the grassy clifftop towards the edge. The sea crashed on the rocks far below.

The wind whipped my hair and tore at the blanket I held around my shoulders. I breathed the smell of the sea. I loved that smell, and I love it still, as long as I am safe on land. Lavinia followed me. I went as close to the edge as I dared. I looked out over the sea, shaky from too little sleep and from the cold and the fear of not finding my name.

Just at that moment, the wind dropped, the sea calmed, the waves became smaller and the crested white horses were fewer and fewer. Suddenly there was a new movement in the water: three dolphins, those rare visitors, dark loops arching in and out of the waves. As we watched them they leapt and splashed. Then they were gone.

Now I know your name, said Lavinia, her dear wise face smiling at me in delight.

Marina, she said (in our way). She of the sea. Sea-born woman.

I am afraid of the sea, I said. How can that be my name?

The dolphins saluted you, she replied. Their message is clear. The sea is your destiny, even if you fear it. And you fear it with reason.

She did not know, and nor did I, what seawater destiny Broccomagus was already planning for me.

The sun sank, the sky grew red, and she said, Let us go, the vigil is over. We will eat now.

The next morning, I received the tattoo around my wrist that marks me as one of my people. It also contains a symbol of my name. In the curving lines are the shapes of dolphins and seals swimming. The design runs in a circle, like a fence around a village. But not a complete circle. There is a break on the inside of my wrist where you can see the blue veins branching down into my palm. The circle is left open. The lifeblood must flow through the gate.

Lavender's blue, dilly dilly,
Lavender's green . . .
> —Nursery rhyme

The word we use in English for the ancient custom of the *tattoo* was imported from the Pacific peoples in the eighteenth century. Yet this custom, as Marina confirms, existed among the Iron Age inhabitants of the place later called England.

Marina's choice of the word *stigmata*, the Latin word for markings made by puncturing the skin and inserting dye, shows that the designs on her wrist were not merely painted on the surface of the skin. This is valuable evidence in the old debate over whether ancient Britons were painted or tattooed or both.

Julius Caesar said the Britons were blue with woad; he used the word *caeruleus* for blue, and since woad still grows and craftspeople still make dye from it, we can see that it does indeed yield the colour blue. But Latin sources in general show that the boundaries between blue and green were different for Latin speakers than for us. *Caeruleus*, or *caerulus*, comes from the word for "heaven" and so has been applied to skies and seas, but also watermelon and cucumbers; while *viridis* has described not only grass and trees but also sea and sky. Then there is *glaucus*, apparently meaning greenish, light green, blue-green, or grey-blue; and *thalassinus*, sea-green, from Greek *thalassa*, sea.

Welsh, and presumably the ancient British language from which it came, is one of the many languages without a distinction between blue and green; *glas* covers many shades of blue and green, and blue-green, and grey; the colour of the sea, and of the sky; of grass and of silver.

When Marina, a native speaker of ancient British who is writing in Latin, says something is *viridis* or *caeruleus* or *glaucus*, we cannot see exactly the shade she sees.

Can we ever see things as another person sees them? What did Marina see in her mind's eye when she thought of her native land? The beginnings of new towns, perhaps, with the stone still fresh from the quarry; villages of round thatched huts, and the clifftop stronghold of her people behind its banks and palisades.

Or perhaps, in the word "home," she saw just one small thing; one patch of shingle on the beach, one dimple in the hillside with a clump of furze. But whatever she saw, it must have had a significance for her that I cannot imagine. The woods were haunted by the supernatural, the river waters rippled with nymphs.

And yet surely the landscape was not so different then? The high cliffs, the trees in the valleys, and fields for horses and sheep; the same tender green in spring; the same seagulls in the air, and elusive seals in the sea. There were many of the same wild flowers—coltsfoot, bluebells in the woods filling the air with their intense blue-green aroma.

At last I am beginning to recognize my own long-buried homesickness, which my short-term visits have never been able to assuage. But I am too ill in body to leave here now, and I rely too much on my doctor, and the treatment. I have left it too late: and now I will never see England again.

Soon after the ides of November.

The remembering is faster and faster now.

As we weave the blanket for Tilla's baby, I think of weaving with my mother. As Glauca and I pick the last of the herbs to store for winter, I think of the plants my mother dried for warm drinks on cold winter nights, plants of my own country with names I do not know in Latin.

I tell Tilla some of the things I remember. She tells me a little about her girlhood. When she arrived at the house of her uncle as a little child, she was terrified. She did not know what had happened to her parents, or why she had been taken from her own nurse. But she loved Baucylia after a while, and was comforted by the kindness of her aunt, Flavia Domitilla.

If only Flavia Domitilla were with us now.

We have sent letters to her on Pandateria in secret, by fishermen and merchants. We have not received even one reply. I think those letters never reached her. Perhaps the fishermen and merchants betrayed us and gave them to the guards. Otherwise why has she not answered even the letter saying Tilla is pregnant?

After the ides of November.

This has been a day of bitterness.

The guards came, bearing bad news for us. We have had a request, they said, from some Christians visiting Pandateria. They want permission to come here, they want to tell you about something that has happened.

And the soldiers paused so we had time to think about this. Time to become frightened.

At last they said: Flavia Domitilla is dead.

They watched Tilla as she struggled to maintain her composure. They said perhaps the visit would be allowed, perhaps not. Then they left.

Tilla wept inconsolably and so did I. Just knowing the lady Flavia Domitilla was there, on the island we can sometimes see, has helped us feel she was with us. As Tilla wept, she began saying, "It's my fault, it's my fault." I put my arms around her saying of course it is not her fault. Then, she stopped crying, and suddenly she was telling me everything.

She told me how, in the house in Rome, servants of the emperor came sometimes from his part of the palace to ours and escorted her to his rooms. Her attendants were bribed to silence.

At first she said nothing to anyone. And, at first, she liked it.

Can you understand, Marina, she said to me now, it began with kindness. He was so kind to me.

She was proud to be singled out by him. She was, in the beginning, too young to understand what use he wanted to make of her. He pampered her and praised her beauty. He fed her delicacies and delicious drinks. It was all the more cruel, then, when he became violent and brutal. She did not tell me exactly what he did, but I saw the horror in her face. Where before she had longed for their meetings, now she dreaded them. Her whole life was full of fear that the emperor would send for her again.

She poured all this out in a rush of words.

Every time they took her there, she told herself that it was surely the last time. Whenever she came back, she tried to forget what happened in his rooms. Her aunt, busy and a little absent-minded as usual, knew only that the emperor liked Tilla. That he sometimes sent for her, as a mark of special favour. But, at last, Flavia Domitilla noticed Tilla's unhappiness and made her explain it.

My aunt did not blame me, Tilla said, I was so afraid of that. She blamed only him.

When Tilla told me this I loved the lady Flavia Domitilla more than ever.

I remembered how Domitianus, when Tilla stood before him pleading, had stared at her breasts and thighs under her robe. How she had avoided his eyes one minute, and the next looked at him with a surprising familiarity and contempt.

Now I understand: this was why he killed his cousin Flavius Clemens and banished Flavia Domitilla. Not only, not even primarily, because of their interest in the strange philosophies of the Jews and Christians. Not because of the way Flavius Clemens neglected the ceremonies due to the gods and the genius of the emperor. It was because Flavius Clemens and his wife had discovered the secret game Domitianus was playing with Tilla, and they went to him in anger and tried to make him stop.

Now Tilla cried, Why was I so weak? If only I had just kept on as I was, bearing it alone. But I was so afraid of him.

She sobbed.

I have their blood on my hands, she said. I killed them both.

Since the arrest of Flavius Clemens, the girl has carried this guilt.

Later today Tilla said, Here, at last, on this island, I have been starting to believe he has forgotten me. I, a prisoner, feel free.

But now, what if the guards tell him about—she laid a hand on the small bulge of her belly—about this?

I reassured her that they probably had not seen it when they were here. Folds of fabric still hide her shape.

We both wanted to wash at the end of this day. We helped each other as we have done before. It shocked me the first time she wanted to help me, as I had helped her. Now I am used to it. Everything is different here.

She had said, In Rome I thought I could do nothing for myself. But I can. The girl Chloë has too much work already. And you are no slave.

That first time she took the scoop, laughing, and poured the water over me so naturally that my shyness at her serving me washed away with the dirt.

So today we filled the braziers with charcoal to take the chill from the air. We used water the boys brought up from the cistern in buckets, and warmed in the kitchen. The bathhouse fires are lit only rarely.

She is still thin everywhere except for her growing belly and her breasts with their large dark circles. I watched the water run over them and spread outwards over the curved belly, and down her legs. They have hair on them now, because she does not have anyone to depilate them for her.

Of course I have not taken any trouble over my own for a long time.

I am remembering Cosmas, the way he ran his hands down my thighs, the way he touched me when he still seemed to care for me. I wonder if she thinks of the hands of the emperor on her skin, over her flesh, on thigh and nipple, and if there is any pleasure in the memory, or only revulsion.

Her belly grows and grows, with its brown stripe down the middle. Like an apricot. Is it strange for her to see in her body the swelling fruit of the emperor's seed?

_In my grandFather's dayes, the Manuscripts flew about like Butter-
flies. All Musick bookes, Account-bookes, Copie books, etc, were covered with old Manuscripts, as we cover them now with blew Paper,
or Marbled Paper. And the Glovers at Malmesbury made great
Havock of them, and Gloves were wrapt up no doubt in many good
pieces of Antiquity._

—John Aubrey

Those who know Rome know the name Domitilla because of
the Catacomb of Domitilla on the Via Ardeatina, just south of
the old city wall. This catacomb seems to have been named not
after someone buried there, but after the owner of the original
land. Old records speak of burials on the _praedium domitillae_, the
estate of Domitilla, and an ancient inscription shows that a Flavia
Domitilla had granted permission for burials on her estate, but
not which of the several women of that name she was. Other inscriptions specify that a Flavia Domitilla, granddaughter of Ves-
pasian, gave land for burials, but in those cases it is not clear
which piece of land. The limited number of names among ancient
Romans leads to confusion, especially for the lives of women. Sisters often had the same exact name, based on their father's, and
were called "older" and "younger" to distinguish them.

I wanted a new name for my new life here in America. I chose
"Aubrey" because I liked the sound of it; I liked its antiquarian
ring, its evocation of a nineteenth-century scholar or clergyman.
I liked that it is (or was then) a man's name; make of that what
you will. There was the added bonus of paying homage to John
Aubrey, with whose passion for the disappearing remnants of
the past I sympathized, and still do. But my new name increased
my feeling of being a stranger. My voice, like Marina's tattoo,
already marked me out as foreign. Then I unthinkingly made
things worse by choosing a name people here say differently from
the way I say it myself.

This is the first time that I have spoken, or written, about my
change of name. Until I began these pages I had never disclosed

any part of my early life. The two halves of my shell are cracking open; my carapace is falling away.

I think of Marina opening her book, turning to the place where she last wrote, dipping her pen in the ink, enacting the ritual of writing, as I am doing in this book of mine. When I copy out Marina's manuscript, I echo her work, her hand's journey across the parchment.

It was not easy for me to adjust to America. This is difficult to explain to immigrants who have come from countries with other languages or non-western ways; they think, as I thought before I arrived, that speaking English and being born in the same land as the founding fathers would give an English newcomer a sense of home. But instead, I felt a deep and disconcerting alienation, as if in a dream of a known world but with everything shifted just a little off kilter.

Familiar things had different names, and no one understood me unless I used the new word; other things bore familiar names used in strange ways: a "robin" here is not a real robin, but a kind of thrush. And it was more than the linguistic differences. Everything, as is so often said by new arrivals, is bigger in America—milk cartons (and no bottles on the doorstep either), cars (especially then), refrigerators. Everything except the banknotes, or "bills," which were very small, and all coloured the same muddy green.

I wanted to be an estate agent, and the first thing I had to learn was to call myself a "real estate agent"; and I had to show houses enthusiastically as if the strangest things were desirable—open-plan rooms with no books or bookshelves, exposed gardens ("yards") with no fences or walls between them and no privacy at all. The houses were lovely and big, it must be said. I drove (on the wrong side of the road, but luckily this was not too hard as I had never driven in England) from house to house, township to township (often without any real towns), learning the way and the language and the look of things and what people wanted, and I had to keep my head above water in the strangeness of it all.

Yet if I caught myself indulging self-pity, I clamped down on it; I had no right, when so many refugees could never return to their native lands, and had lost people they loved, whole families even. My small losses were nothing. I had chosen to come, after all.

I was always being asked to explain myself. Where are you from? Are you Irish, Australian, or British? Why are you here? Is all your family here too? And then the unspoken questions—married? But there's no ring. A spinster, then?

Of course I don't really think many Americans looked at me and used this word in their minds. But when I was in my twenties and thirties, people here were still marrying very young. Sometimes, tired of people's puzzled faces, I thought that I might put some sort of ring on the fourth finger of my left hand. But I didn't and don't care much for jewelry, and anyway, why should people's questions matter? I am not married, and have never been, and that is that.

Did I ever love anyone enough to want to marry him? Yes. Once. But he did not want to marry me.

I'm trying to face this truth: I have made a mess of my life. If you could hear my voice saying those words—still after all these years sounding somewhat English, and with that jokey self-deprecation—you'd think perhaps I didn't mean it. That's how we disguise our despair.

As I look back, I have that feeling that comes over you at the end of a day you've wasted for no good reason: you can't believe you let all those hours slip by. Only for me it's not the hours of a day, it's not even a mere week; it's a whole life, my one and only, my finite, life.

What have I to show for it? A few schoolchildren have chosen to benefit from my instruction. I've researched the ancient past a little. Transcribing and translating Marina's book is the most important work I have ever done, and it has been tainted by secrecy.

I have a garden, but no one to share it with. Not that I think finding a life partner is the sole aim of living. But who will sit beside me as I wonder if my time on earth will have made the slightest difference to anything or anyone? Who will help me to accept that it must end so soon? No one. I must sit beside myself, I must help myself accept.

Just after the kalends of December.

It is the season of closed seas. Most of the fishing boats have been pulled up into a large cave below this house, near the eel pools, where they are protected. Not all of them: one foolhardy fisherman, a young man, kept his boat on the water and went out with two companions. They were caught in a storm. All are believed lost. Their bodies have not yet washed ashore. Octavius is not in the kitchen today, for one of them was a relative of his. Chloë cries all the time. She was to marry another of these boys. The sea has taken so many of the people of this island, as it took so many of my own place.

A terrible death, says Tilla, out there on the sea.

That was nearly my death, I say.

And now, here in this place where neither of us belongs, I have told Tilla my story.

I told her how that spring the fish were not running, the particular silver-blue fish (I do not know the Latin name) which sustained us more than any other food at that time of year. And the grain stored in the ground was already used up, earlier than usual, for the previous harvest had been poor.

The new lambs jumped in the fields. The yellow spring flowers had come and gone. The boat festival grew near. We used to send the year's first boat out on the water, full of flowers, as a gift to the sea. And after that the fishermen could safely embark on the first big expedition of the season.

On the evening before the festival, my father and brother were with the other men making preparations. My mother and I and my little sister, who had only lived three winters, were in our house. I was practising my letters by rushlight, sadly, because the teacher Cosmas was going away.

Then Broccomagus came to the door with Alauna, the priestess who had conducted the prayers of my new womanhood. We admitted them. My mother offered a warm drink, and they accepted. Broccomagus held his cup tensely and looked at me. He said I was to have a special part to play in the festival the next day, and they must take me now, that very evening, to the sacred place. I heard my mother sharply draw in her breath.

The priestess said to me, Give me your mirror. Something in my mother's face as I put the mirror into Alauna's hands made me shiver. My mother said, I will come with her.

No, said Broccomagus, but you will see her later tonight.

As we walked towards the beach, Alauna asked me, You have not been lying with any boys in the woods, have you?

It seemed she was teasing. Yet she spoke as if it were important. And I said, truthfully, no. Not adding how much I had dreamt of it.

By the boats were several men and women, talking quite loudly, even angrily. All fell silent when they saw me. The priestess led me to the door of the house of preparation. She put her hand on my shoulder and said loudly to them all:

Here is the sea-chosen girl. She has had her first blood, but not her first man. She is a woman, yet not a woman. She will be our gift to the sea.

Yes, the old way! a voice said. Broccomagus cried, Silence! The Romans must not know of it.

My aunt Lavinia was there. She stepped forward, and said to Broccomagus:

It was not for this that the dolphins saluted her. This is not the meaning of her name. I saw a different destiny.

Then the priestess pushed me through the door and I could not hear his answer. I did not understand anything of what was happening.

I had never been inside the preparation house. This was where priests put on their robes and crowns before ceremonies. The priestess and another woman made me sit in a tall wicker chair. They treated me like a great lady, a queen. They draped me with heavy robes and gold bracelets. They pinned the robes with silver brooches in the shapes of hare and boar and dog and horse and fish and dolphin, covering me with protection and honour. There was a warm fire, and food, and mead, and herbs. I grew sleepy, and they led me to a couch covered in richly dyed wools.

Lavinia came in and sat down beside the couch, took my hands, and spoke words of courage to me. I did not understand why she seemed angry, not with me, but about what was being done. Then my mother, father, brother and little sister appeared. Why did my father's face look so strange? Why was my mother crying? Why did she hold me tightly, and kiss me?

Why did my father say to Broccomagus, This is forbidden now. You know they will punish us all.

And what did the answer of Broccomagus mean? He said, Better the Roman punishment than the punishment of the gods for abandoning the old ways of our people.

And he spoke mockingly to my father, saying, Leave now, soft old man. You have forgotten how things should be done. You are fortunate that she has been chosen.

And then my family was taken away, my little sister sucking her thumb, bewildered, and my mother turning to look back at me with that anguished face.

I was alone with the priestess who sat with her herbs and infusions in little bags and pots. The fire crackled. The mirror lay on the couch beside my head. It would be given to the sea with me. Outside, mixed with the sound of the wind and of the waves gnawing at the foot of the cliff, I heard a clinking of metal: the trappings of my horse. She was tethered there because she too would die at dawn. The horses of the sea would call to her, come galloping, sweep over her, and take her into their wild company for ever.

Soon I stopped feeling afraid: as if it was all a tale about someone else from long ago. Perhaps this was a mercy of the herbs. I looked at the mirror, the swirling lines on its back. I turned it over and stared at my face in it. A stranger's face. I fingered the rich red cloth of the dress they had put on me. I was proud that

I was the chosen one. I thought of all the stories I ever knew about the distant islands where the dead go. I would drift over the water and find the heroes and grandmothers where they live and feast, for ever young, and there is no bitter wind. The herbs kept my mind from thinking about the drowning, the water-death, the casting-off of the first boat according to the old way of our ancestors.

Next day.

I want to tell it to the end, now I have begun, as I told it all to Tilla.

High in the wall of the house of preparation, there was a small opening. There I saw the light of dawn in the sky.

Broccomagus and Alauna came for me. They were robed, crowned, singing, carrying branches of hazel.

They told me to bring the mirror, holding it high as I walked: it flashed in the strengthening light. People were standing silent along the path. Others were massed on the shingle. There was an early morning mist, chilly air.

The boat was ready. It was decorated with early spring flowers and leaves, bright-coloured cloths were draped over the sides, and it had a sail with patterns I had never seen before.

The boat had no oars.

The salt wind cleared my hazy mind, and my heart beat faster. I began to feel the sharpness of fear.

Broccomagus lifted his arm to the heavens, his sleeve fell back revealing the blue eel-like twistings etched there. His powerful words rang out over the waves:

He said, She has come willingly to the place. Here she is, pre-pared and ready, a precious life in a worthy boat, the sacred boat that all will know from its colours and that no one may touch once it is cast off. It is given to the sea to go wherever the sea will take it. The sea will accept our offering and send us fish again. The waves will be thick with the silver skeins of fish. They will swim into our nets, and we shall eat. We shall have strength to work our fields. Our women will bear children, and the land will give us grain.

Then he pointed his long arm and finger at me, and he screamed out the curse, the banishment. If the boat should somehow wash up on another shore, I must never come back. If I tried, all the pebbles of all the beaches would burn my soles, the water of all the wells would burn my throat, because I did not belong to my land any more. I had been given to the sea. I could never be received again by that land or by my people. And if I did return, the people had the right to kill me.

His words were shrieked out onto the wind like the cry of a raven of doom.

Then his voice fell silent.

The sea was rough that morning, but the wind was good for the sacrifice, it would carry the boat away from the shore. They helped me into the boat, made me sit on the single bench. They put a wreath of spring flowers on my head, and the mirror on my thighs. On the floor of the boat were placed a black bowl with food in it, a spoon, and a stoppered pouch full of mead.

They cast the boat off, it rocked on the waves, the men pushed it out into the sea, wading beside me. I saw their jaws and hair, the skin of their muscled arms incised blue with the patterns of my people. None of them looked into my face. The outgoing tide took the boat, and the wind caught the sail. The men let it go.

I saw them lead my horse to the edge of the sea and tie her to a stake. She whinnied with terror.

I was alone. I turned away and stared out at the horizon. The morning light was growing stronger. I took the spoon and ate the porridge in the burnished black bowl, tasting the hazelnuts in it. They were the food of life to sustain me until I reached the other world. Then I sipped the mead. I drank and wept and waited for it to dull my senses. I kept looking back at the now-distant coastline. After a while I could no longer distinguish the cliff where my namestone was hidden, or see our cove, or my horse.

I do not know how much time went by. The boat rocked up
and down, the wind filling the sail, the water slapping against
the hull's greased leather skin. The seasickness grew and grew.
There was a grey world of cold water all around me. The waves
were never-ending. I was completely alone in them, except for
the seagulls. Every so often a large wave came and crashed water
into the boat, and I scooped it out a little at a time with the porridge bowl. Before I could finish, another would come, and I had
to scoop even more. My feet and hands were ice cold. I was weak
and shivering. I pulled the cloak around me and pinned the
brooches tight, but the wind still came through. I began to hope
for death.

After a long long span, I saw three dolphins, their black bodies
shining as they played alongside the boat for a while. Were they
the same ones we saw on the naming day? Their companion-
ship cheered me. Even if they had come to take me to the other
world, I was glad of them.

And then suddenly something large was near, looming high.
A ship, a trading ship of the people across the water, returning
to their land. It came closer and closer until I thought it would
run me down. As I watched in terror I heard men shouting,
the words lost in the wind at first. Then I heard, incredibly, my
name. I could see the faces of the men on deck high above me.
And there with them was the tutor Cosmas. A rope ladder was
let down and Cosmas sent two sailors. They were praying loudly
in their fear of the holy coracle that no one could touch. They
helped me climb out of my boat and up to theirs. It was difficult. Although I had pulled off the heavy outer robes, I was grip-
ping the mirror so tightly in one hand that the bronze loops of
the handle left marks on my palm afterwards. At last I was sitting on the deckboards of the trading ship.

Bewildered, dazed, I could not understand anything. Cosmas
put his arms around me: a circle of warmth and strength.

He told me that, while I was in the preparation hut, my mother
had gone to him for help. She knew he was sailing the next day,
because too many of the people had listened to Broccomagus

and he was forced to leave. She had begged him to search the sea for the boat with no oars.

He said, She gave me this for you.

It was the cloth she had been weaving, with threads the colours of the sea and the sky, the one that was to be a cloak for me. She had taken it off the loom small and unfinished. She gave him words for me too: Guard the mirror well. And guard your life.

I wrapped the cloth around the mirror, it was just big enough to enfold the mirror twice and keep it safe.

I spent the journey in the ship with the knowledge that I was cast out from my own place and people. I had been sent away from my father and mother and all I had ever known. And I could never go back. In the coracle I had been in terror of death in the maw of a seamonster or under a wave. I had tried to hope for the land of the ever-young. Now, instead, there was this exile, and a ship taking me somewhere unknown, far from my own country. Was it good to be alive but exiled? Or would exile be more terrible than death?

Near the Gallic shore, Cosmas put his hand, heavy, warm, over my hand, as he had done when first guiding it to shape the letters.

He said, Come with me. Be my companion, and learn my work.

I had nowhere to go. I was alone but for him; what else could I do?

Close by were the Druids, lifting their hands to heaven and pouring forth dreadful curses . . . their groves, consecrated to their savage superstitions, were destroyed. Piety for them meant drenching their altars in the blood of prisoners and consulting their gods by means of human entrails.

—Tacitus, *Annals*

Roman writers spoke of human sacrifice among the Gauls and Britons, as Tacitus does in this description of druid worship on the island of Anglesey, then called Mona. Archaeology has yielded the proof. Remains of bodies of infants, children, men and women have been found in grain-storage pits, in building foundations, under hillforts, in bogs and in many other places. They were killed in different ways and their bodies subjected to grisly mutilations before and after death.

Spanish witnesses who lived alongside the people in South America wrote of the seasonal rituals involving human sacrifice; sometimes the victim was a prisoner of war, at other times a child or children, or a young woman, or a young man chosen a year earlier and pampered for months until the moment he willingly climbed the steps to the sacrificial altar. For Iron Age Britain and continental Europe we have sparse records from observers and none from the people themselves. We do not know what it meant, for example, when in northwest Britain a young man of aristocratic physique, with a fox fur band around his upper arm, was garroted, hit on the head, drowned, and left in a bog, to be found about 2000 years later. This is Lindow Man, and the salvaged part of his peat-tanned leathery body is now under glass in the British Museum.

If we give to the gods, they will give in return, and bless our harvests and our health. And when we are blessed with fertility, we offer the first fruits and the most precious creatures, even our children, in awe and gratitude. But we must not anger the gods; sometimes the member of a community commits a fatal offence, and then a sacrifice is necessary to cleanse the people.

We consider ourselves so civilized now.

I was sent away because I was a transgressor. My fertility was at the wrong time, in the wrong place; a sin. My mother could not bear the shame of keeping me at home, unmarried, swelling, the advertisement of her own failure to bring me up correctly. She made other arrangements.

She did not come with me to the maternity home; it was quite far away, in a town by the sea. She saw me to the coach station, and, in a wordless gesture towards my health and my baby's, she carried my bag. She gave it to the driver to put in the hold while I climbed onto the bus and sat down. I looked out of the window;

she saw where I was sitting, and gave a brisk wave; I waved back as she walked away, and the bus engine roared, mixing my pain and confusion with acrid fumes.

Some days before the ides of December.

These are days of wind and a cold hard rain. Long and dark.

If it is light enough in the mornings, Tilla and I work on weaving and on sewing clothes for the baby. The lamps must be used sparingly now.

We have been eating every day the pickled greens Glauca made earlier this spring, samphire and parsley and alexanders. She takes them from a great jar stoppered with a mass of fluffy dried fennel, just like the jars we have helped her prepare. Those we will probably be opening before the winter is over.

When the clouds clear, if we go outside at night and look into the sky, we can see the seven sisters now, the seven daughters of the sea, in their cluster like foam on a wave. Glauca knows tales of them, a little different from the ones I know.

During winter nights in my childhood, while mending nets and spinning wool, or twisting threads to make cord and braid, the old people told stories. They used to say to us children, This is what my grandfather, or grandmother, told me when I was a child like you. Listen well, remember it well. You will tell this story to your children and your children's children.

Who will hear the stories from me? And they have faded in my mind now. I am too far away from the place where those stories belong.

On dark winter nights when I was a child we made lamps of scallop shells with fish oil: small indoor stars.

Now as we sit indoors, trying to keep warm with the heat from the braziers, the wind outside howls.

A few days before the ides of December.

It is strangely mild, there is a break in the rain and cold. We walk on the terraces, look out over the sea, feel hope for the spring.

Glauca fears for the fishermen. She knows that in this weather they will take their boats out, despite the deaths there have already been. The sea and the skies can change in an instant.

The ides of December.

We have visitors.

There are three of them: a man and two women.

They came in a boat from Pandateria that ventured across the winter seas because of this mild spell. Although we never believed it would happen, they have been given permission to bring us news of Flavia Domitilla.

They are from Tarracina on the mainland. They went in spring to Pandateria, to visit the Christians banished there with Flavia Domitilla. They stayed all summer and even after the closing of the seas, until Flavia Domitilla died. Now they have come here from Pandateria, from one prison island to another, to bring Tilla news of her aunt.

Her last words were, Take my embrace to Tilla, and my greetings to Marina.

She had lost heart after the death of her baby and had no strength to fight her sickness. She longed for her children in Rome and for Tilla. She had received all the letters Tilla sent with fishermen and traders, and read them again and again. By a refined cruelty the guards would not permit her, or the Christians banished with her, to have any pens or parchment, styli or tablets, or to send any letters off the island. This made her despair, especially when she received our letter about Tilla's pregnancy.

The visiting Christians promised to come to Pontia. She died in the comfort of this promise.

They have brought with them her copy of the book of Loukas. The woman named Dorothea gave Tilla the scroll her aunt had touched, and Tilla pressed it to her heart, weeping. The man, Lucius, told us that Flavia Domitilla would have become a Christian like them if she had lived. She even gave the Christians of Rome permission to bury their dead on the piece of her land where the nurse Baucylia, other servants, and family members had already been buried.

The woman called Zoë opened a bundle she was carrying, and said to Tilla, these are for you. One by one, she took out tiny garments and swaddling cloths and showed them to Tilla, piled them in her lap.

We and other women made them for your baby, she said.

Tilla stared in amazement, touching the little shirts and leggings delicately, reverently, with her long slim fingers. Lucius watched smiling, as we exclaimed over the clothes, so small, so finely sewn.

Dorothea said, When your last letter arrived, Flavia Domitilla was more unhappy than ever not to be able to see you, or even write to you. If only you knew, Tilla, how many tears this caused her. We wanted you to have the things you need for your child.

Zoë, the other woman, who is a midwife, sent Lucius away and put her hand on Tilla's belly. With her fingers she felt the body of the baby under Tilla's skin.

Here are the buttocks, she said, touching the bulge up against Tilla's ribs.

The head is down as it should be. Soon it will drop. And here's a foot—and even as she pressed gently, the baby inside moved, and we all laughed.

Another few days later.

Lucius eats a simple thing—a boiled egg, a piece of cheese—as if it were food of the gods. The woman called Dorothea does not stop chattering, talks merrily of this and that. Zoë is more serious, with a heavy body and a heavy, steady way about her too.

Tilla asked her, Why send yourself into exile? Do you not miss your homes, your families, when you travel like this?

Zoë said, We do. But this is the work we are called to. In Tarracina we heard that there were Christians exiled on Pandateria. We had to go there. And there we came to love your aunt, and promised her we would come to Pontia, to you.

Lucius added, We try not to burden ourselves with husbands or wives, and children. Marriage is not evil: but some of us, especially those who travel as we do, are meant to be free of it. Though sometimes I miss the comforts it might bring.

He smiled. Did I imagine that he caught my eye?

I know Dorothea and Zoë are widows with grown children. They are much older than he is. He seems about thirty-five years old. Has he never married anyone?

Dorothea added, And as for homes, we have no true home in this world. Our country is in another place. We are in exile everywhere.

That is surely sad, said Tilla.

No, replied Zoë: for the Spirit of Iesous is always with us, wherever we go. Because of him, we belong to the household of God.

They tell us about how their way of following Iesous has spread, how there are groups in all the cities. They can travel from Christian house to Christian house. They can find help and friendship even among strangers. It is Iesous who connects us all, says Zoë.

Next day. Saturnalia.

Today Zoë sat by me for a while. Dorothea and Lucius were talking to Tilla. Zoë has square, stubby fingers, strong and capable. She was eating an apple, taken from the wooden chests where we keep them out of the air. She turned it carefully as she peeled it.

She looked at me as if she cared for me the way a sister or mother would.

She asked about the last days in the household of Flavius Clemens.

Flavia Domitilla had spoken of it a little before she died. But Zoë asked what I remember.

I told her how foolishly I followed Tilla when she went to confront the emperor, how I did not hold her back. And how many times I have longed to undo that moment.

Zoë's amber eyes looked into mine as she said:

There is a reason Tilla is here and you are here with her. Perhaps it will only come to light after a long time has passed.

The others had stopped talking for a moment and her words fell into the silence. They all turned to look at us. In the faces of Lucius and Dorothea I saw complete trust in Zoë's wisdom.

Then Lucius added:

Yes, this is the place where you are meant to be now: but only for a while. Then, you must go home.

I did not speak the question that was in my mind: where is home?

Another day of Saturnalia.

The Christians are strange. They do not give gifts for Saturnalia, or share in any of the celebrations. The house has been in an uproar with feasts as fine as Glauca can make them, and music and singing. Slaves have enjoyed their brief imitation of liberty. But Lucius and the women have kept themselves away from all that.

Yet I like to listen to Lucius when he talks. He tells how he prays in the name of Iesous and his prayers are heard. How he sometimes knows things through the spirit of Iesous. I watch and listen and I almost believe. He tells of the courage and deeds of Paulos, he tells of dying people healed and of shipwrecks averted, all by the power of Iesous.

Perhaps Iesous has indeed become a god, and can heal, as the Lady Isis does, and other gods. Lucius says demons mislead us by illusion, and Isis and Apollo and Asclepius are mere lifeless statues. Yet I have seen people healed by them. And what of the gods that keep Rome strong, Capitoline Jupiter to whom the noblest bulls are sacrificed, and Vesta in whose nostrils the virgins' incense burns night and day? Are they not pleased, is this not why Rome wins battle after battle?

Surely the gods choose whom they will help: and they chose not to help me. The Lady Isis, the gods of Rome with their high-pillared temples, the gods of every place where I have made offerings, they all dismissed my prayers and vows. I do not belong anywhere.

In my land there was power on the hillsides, in the wind, among the sacred trees of my ancestors. But now I am too far away from the gods of my own place.

Isis the Great Mother, Great Saviour, she of the sea, she who searched in the waters for her beloved Osiris for three days until she found him and brought him back to life, I turn to her still, I long for her care and her protection. But I do not think she has room beneath her mantle for a *peregrina*, a foreigner like me.

Lucius says Iesous is for people from any land, Jew, Greek, Roman, free or slave. And Iesous the Nazarene is a foreigner in Italy, as much as I am. Even in his own land he was a wanderer and had nowhere to lay his head.

Praise for the sweetness
of the wet garden
sprung in completeness
where his feet pass.

—Eleanor Farjeon, *Morning Song*

They say there are no atheists in foxholes. I am in a foxhole, and naturally I want to believe there is "something." I want this not to be the end of me, of my consciousness. I want to believe in the light at the end of the tunnel that the nearly-dead claim to have seen, I want to believe there is a loving welcome waiting for me. But these reports are tenuous; and even the Anglican faith of my childhood, in all its beauty and poetry, seems flimsy to sustain me now.

Far more than England, with its abandoned country churches and their silenced bells, America is a land of churchgoers, but I do not join them. I do not go to church. Sometimes at Christmas and Easter I have attended for the sake of tradition.

Growing up where the stones of the churches have seen centuries of worship and absorbed the voices of countless singers, I could not help finding reassurance in the antiquity of the faith. I did feel something, year after year in church with my mother all my childhood, listening to the prayers of the repeated seasons, hearing poetry over and over again.

He does not crush the broken reed, nor quench the wavering flame.

The hymns that moved me most, at church, and at the convent school where I was one of the non-Catholic girls, were those that expressed and intensified what I already felt, that God was immanent in hills, trees, the sea. And in a dew-drenched garden, with the blackbird singing.

Here, there is no blackbird song. Eleanor Farjeon's words evoked an English morning so perfectly then, when I was there; so poignantly now that I am not. And the spiritual place where I might feel every morning is like the first morning of creation— that is another country where I cannot live.

In the maternity home, religion was thrust upon us, we who were guilty and shameful because of our sullied condition. Forgiveness could be ours, yes; but at a price. They preached at us often, but in my bag I had packed an anthology of poetry, and while waiting for the baby I was more comforted by the poems than by any religious instruction.

But once the baby came, and I loved her, and then lost her, nothing could comfort me. Since then, the spiritual impulses of my youth have not reappeared, except in my response to the natural world. If there were a Higher Power, and in the unlikely event it wanted to speak to me, I might be more ready to listen by the waters of the river, or where the wind rushes through the trees, or in my garden contemplating the fragrant layers of the first peony. But I would probably still assume I imagined it.

Clearly I am not by any measure spiritually prepared, if this is indeed—as it absurdly seems to be—the end of my life. And it would be unseemly to try and find God now, in a frenzied search, like scrabbling in a handbag for a lost bus ticket as the bus prepares to depart. But there is one thing I can do. It is difficult.

I no longer have the luxury of returning to England when I am ready, and gradually easing myself into an encounter with the past, glancing tentatively at my mistakes. Now I must meet them head-on, especially the biggest mistake of all.

So I must undergo a conversion, turn myself inside-out from the person I have been, who has kept everything buried all this time: and simply (if it were only simple!) reach back into the past and unearth the whole of my story. And I must write it down, for it is all I have to give.

Another day near the end of December.

I do not often take out this book while the visitors are here.

Tilla listens to the talk about Iesous and asks questions, her face alive with interest. She is eager to learn more of the mysteries of he whom they name the Anointed One, the Christos. But they cannot be told to the uninitiated.

She asks, When can I be really one of you?

They answer, Not yet. After a while.

I watch Lucius, his eyes alive, his hands with their blisters and calluses moving quickly as he speaks, his whole body awake. And mine awake, watching him.

He told us that he was named for Loukas, the companion of Paulos, he who wrote the book they gave Flavia Domitilla and then Tilla. Paulos and Loukas stayed a little while at Tarracina while on their way from Puteoli to Rome. Lucius, who was born in Tarracina, was a child then, and he had a different name. At that time he was very ill. He was so ill that all the doctors told his mother he would soon die. But she brought him to Paulos and Loukas, because she had heard of their healing power. Loukas healed him, not only with his skill as a physician, but through the power of Iesous. And so his grateful parents changed his name to Lucius, the Latin form of Loukas, and became followers of the Way.

Lucius believes that Iesous came from the creator god who made everything. The god who sustains the whole world. This is the same god the Jews worship. Iesous came to show us that this god loves not only the Jews but every one of us, all of creation. Our lives are not at the mercy of uncaring destiny, or of battling gods and demons, as it seems. We are in the hands of a loving creator. So Lucius says. The risings and fallings of our fortunes have a meaning. And Iesous can protect us from evil and from demons.

Our visitors have books with them, scrolls they call "the memoirs of the apostles" and "the apostolic teachings," and "the writings of Hermas." They read often from these books. Lucius and Zoë have good memories for finding the piece of writing they want. Dorothea has difficulty, and rolls and unrolls the scroll many times to find the words. It seems to me that a gathering of parchment pages, like these I am writing in, would be simpler for her. I have not spoken of this. It might seem disrespectful of their books.

They tell stories that have been passed down from those who lived and walked with Iesous. I like the story of when he was in a boat with his friends, sleeping, and such a storm blew up that they were all terrified and thought they would die. Yet he slept on. At last they woke him and he calmed the storm. Another time he sent fish swimming to fill the nets after the fishermen had caught nothing all night.

He could easily have stopped the Romans from crucifying him. Yet he chose to die, and went bravely to his death.

End of December.

A few days ago the Christians went down to the harbour and rented lodgings there. Lucius can repair wood and the women can mend clothes and nets, while they tell everyone about their Way.

We said, It is dangerous to speak too openly.

There is no stopping them. They promised to visit us whenever they can. They have already come back once, yesterday. Knowing they are nearby gives us comfort. And because Zoë is a midwife we have less anxiety about the birth.

Tilla and I continue to weave the blanket side by side, as long as the short daylight lasts, and sometimes a little by lamplight too. We want to finish it.

She is a faster weaver than me. I love to watch her long fingers moving deftly between the threads.

Today as we worked we talked about what the Christians said yesterday, that Iesous was truly a man. Some people say he was just spirit and his body was an illusion. But our friends say he was a man who ate and drank and wept. A man who died, shedding real blood.

He did die: but he came back to life, they say. Not as a ghost, but as a flesh-and-blood man again. He still had the wounds in his hands and feet and side. He cooked fish for his friends on the shores of the lake and ate it with them.

Yesterday I asked, If Iesous is alive, where is his place? Of what or where is he the genius?

Dorothea answered, He is not like the little gods of your woods and streams.

Then why do you speak of him as if he is alive? I asked.

Is it that his memory survives among those who admired him?

No, she said, not like that at all. He is really alive. He came back after his death. Mariam of Magdala saw him in the garden. Do not cling to me, he said to her. The others saw him in closed rooms. He appeared, he disappeared, he passed through the walls. No one could hold him. And then he vanished into the sky.

I asked, So he is alive in the sky now?

Yes, but closer than that too. He sent us his spirit. He dwells in many places, wherever his followers are. He is with us always, she said.

I said, I would like to have known him.

Zoë said, you can know him now.

Today Tilla and I remembered all this, especially those words of Zoë's, You can know him now. Tilla said to me as we sat at the loom, What did she mean? How can we know him? I long to know him. She and Dorothea know him, and Lucius. Look at them, look at what it gives them, something I have never seen before.

I agreed. There is something about them that is different.

Lucius said: Iesous is light. Iesous is flowing water.

⁓

Strengthen me with raisins,
refresh me with apples;
for I am faint with love.
　　　　　—*The Bible, Song of Songs*

For a very short while, and only once in my life, my whole religion was love. I adored him, my first lover, the only one I really loved, Franco. He was so beautiful, with the darkness of his curly hair and eyes, his lips like a Botticelli boy's, though he was twenty-six and seemed a man to me then, when I was twenty-two. In a crowded piazza I could immediately pick out his head, his leopard lope, the set of his shoulders. And he seduced me with a straightforward possessiveness that from the beginning said: you are mine.

I was in Rome as part of my Master's degree research and we met when I went with my study group to the church of San Clemente; he was the guide. He took us down through the twelfth-century basilica to the fourth-century church below it, and then to the level under that, with the mithraeum and the first-century house, a house that may have belonged to a family that hosted an early Christian house church, or to Flavius Clemens himself, though that name meant nothing to me then. He spoke adequate but strongly accented English, and everything he said fascinated me, not because of him, at first, but because the place was a palimpsest of over two thousand years; so I stared at him while he spoke, greedily drinking in his words, and he noticed and started directing the words to me, and gradually he himself became as interesting as what he was saying. So afterwards when the group dispersed, I lingered, or found myself lingering without meaning to, or he held me back somehow—I don't know exactly. We went together for a gelato, and that was it; the *colpo di fulmine*. I simply had to yield to it without caution or restraint or the miserly game of playing hard to get. Such a chance, such a man, I knew in my ardent youthfulness, might come along only once in a lifetime.

Over the next few days we wandered among ruins together; he showed me the Forum, we climbed the Palatine hill high above the city, where the traffic noise fades away and you can hear the birds, and there are broken ancient buildings all around. Up there, as we leant side by side against a railing embedded in ancient brickwork, looking down at the shells of what were once the huge rooms of Domitian's palace, he asked,

"Do you like the sea?"

The Roman heat pounded down, and I was weak with it.

"I love the sea," I answered, which was true, and suddenly he stood up straight, turned, leaned his back against the railing and drew me towards him, we kissed long and deeply, he held me so close I could feel his chest and his strong thighs and the strange hardness I had noticed before with boys, and in my inexperience not understood, and he said, looking into my eyes with that dark intensity,

"We go tomorrow, to the sea. To a special *isola*, Ponza."

His certainty of my surrender was irresistible, in a country where so much was unclear and ambiguous, and at a time in my life when I did not know who I was or what I really wanted. My few early boyfriends, with their pallid English faces and tentative ways, their hesitant politenesses, seemed so irrelevant now, so young.

We took the train from Rome to Anzio, and then the ferry to Ponza, a journey long enough for me to feel I was going to another world, a smaller world within the world of Italy. On Ponza we gave our passports to the receptionist of the somewhat shabby *pensione* while I agonized over what she would think, as we were obviously not married, but she paid no attention to that at all, and she gave us the key to our room.

That room is still vivid in my memory. It had a window high in the wall from which you could just see the harbour if you craned your neck sideways. I see the crooked chest of drawers, and the bed, and us on that bed, his body silhouetted against the bright daylight coming through the window, for we could not wait until nightfall.

We spent five days together on Ponza. We walked on the seafront or up and down the tiny flights of stairs between the steep levels—if I was following him, I watched his taut buttocks shifting and I admired his crisp calf muscles as they contracted and relaxed with every stair. We sat in cafes drinking sparkling mineral water, or the island's dry white wine, Fieno, and I looked at his elegant fingers around his glass and thought of what those fingers had just been doing to my skin.

He had been to the island once or twice, years before, and he showed it to me like a gift. We took the boat tour; we swam alone in a natural pool between rocks; we walked in the tunnels that the Romans cut through the steep rock and that are still in use today. One tunnel bores right through the island's high craggy spine. We found the steps leading down to it from a nondescript street, barely signposted, as if it were quite ordinary to have Roman tunnels in one's town. As we walked downwards, the damp tunnel floor, in the same herringbone design of two-thousand-year-old bricks that I saw on the first-century level of San Clemente, sloped away from the entrance, into the dark. Here and there on the walls were traces of *opus reticulatum*, stonework in the diamond net pattern. A little light came in through the roof where the original airholes had collapsed. No one was in the tunnel besides us, and he stopped and gently pushed me over to the wall, and then not so gently stood up right against me, and kissed me, hard, and my back sank into the damp stones until I thought they would print themselves on my skin, as we pressed our mouths and bodies and thighs together until we could hardly breathe or stand. But then we heard people coming, and walked on shakily, until at last the tunnel emerged into the perfect enclosed semicircle of the bay Chiaia di Luna, with its pale sheerly vertical cliffs. The small tide of the Mediterranean had left seaweed and mussel shells across the sand in a wavy dark line, like Roman cursive script.

We went into the tunnel because it was a shortcut to the beach; despite his work in Rome as a guide, Franco was not interested in seeking out traces of the past on Ponza. And I too was living in the present, although I did wonder about the "grotto of Pilate," and Saint Domitilla, and the "cells" that were mentioned on a plaque near the church. I bought a couple of books about the island to read later. He said, "No history now, *cara*. This is holiday. This is our time, our moment."

When he spoke, mostly in English as he wanted to practise, his accented syllables delighted me. And when he said *amore, tesoro, carissima*, I felt infinitely caressed.

The sea was everywhere, catching and holding and multiplying the light.

When the train returned us to the noise and dirt of Rome, we disembarked and arranged to meet for lunch the next day, the last day before I had to leave. Then he went to wherever he lived with his Mamma, and I to my pensione. All the next morning I anticipated a tender, bittersweet meal at our favourite restaurant near the ancient theatre of Marcellus. I knew our imminent parting would overshadow everything, but there would be plans to make—when would he visit me in England? Soon I might see him under the changing English sky, his hair and eyes dramatically dark in that watery air. Or perhaps I would come back to Rome.

We took an outdoor table, and began the ritual, by now so dear to me, of ordering *aqua minerale* (his *naturale*, *gassata* for me), choosing the food, sipping a glass of wine, breathing the complex aroma (*espresso*, *cornetto*, *motorino*) of Rome; and we spoke of trivialities first, I hardly knew what, because I was staring at him so hard, memorizing his face. Then he took my hand across the table—his touch delicate, yet his fingers strong—and looked at me sadly.

"*Carissima*," he said, and I melted inwardly as always when he said this, "*Carissima*, it has been so sweet, this time with you. I shall remember always."

I said, so eager, so hopeful, "But we'll see each other again soon?"

"I think it is not a good idea. My *fidanzata*, she returns next week."

I was flooded with shock, and shame. I thought I was precious to him. He had made me feel sure, without exactly saying so, that we would always be together. Or else it was just my body that felt sure, and pulled my heart along with it: my heart, and my trust.

Yes, it was utterly banal; there was a *fidanzata*, they were to marry the following summer, as their families had planned since they were small. We had swapped places; she was studying English in London. I had not even thought to wonder about such a thing; I assumed he was as free as I was, because he behaved so. Later, of course, I realised there had been clues. He had kept me away from his mother and his circle of friends. And in particular parts of Rome, certain restaurants and streets and piazzas, he behaved with a strange reserve.

I wept helplessly, there at the table. I do not know what else he said, what I said, how it ended. The next day I was back in England.

Then I understood the almost physical agony of that old cliché, a broken heart. I had given so much and been so exquisitely happy that I had no resilience when it all fell to dust. There are people who seem to recover from much more terrible losses; but I never really did.

I had always thought the universe led me to the right places, helped me and guided me. When I met Franco, I thought he was a gift of God and I had been sent to Rome to find him. I thought everything was connected, and there were patterns, and if I kept my eyes open, I could follow the safe path. I thought people were generally honest and trustworthy. I thought I was protected from harm, or I thought that even if a little harm befell me, I would soon be rescued.

Now I had lost Franco, and I had lost that confidence as well.

Some days before the ides of January.

They have left us.

Yesterday, early in the morning, a young man rowed over to the boat landing. He ran up the steps with the news that our friends had been ordered to leave at once, closed seas or not. They talked everywhere about Iesous and his Way and there have been complaints and arguments. Now, just as we feared, the guards have expelled them.

Tilla said to the young man, We will come back to the harbour with you.

I protested that we are forbidden to leave the grounds of this house, but she said, Stay, then, if you are afraid. I must see them one last time.

I went with her.

At the harbour the ship was almost ready to sail. Lucius, Zoë and Dorothea stood near it with their bags, wearing traveling clothes.

We do not want to leave you, said Lucius, But if we disobey this order, we will put you in danger as well. We are not permitted to throw our lives away, and cannot endanger yours.

While the women embraced Tilla, Lucius drew me aside. Suddenly I understood how sorry I was to see him go.

He said, if one day I am in Tarracina, I must seek out his sister at the hot food shop in the street of the silversmiths. She knows where to find him and the other Christians.

Show her this, he said, and he put something warm from his hand into my hand, a piece of tile. He closed my fingers around it before I could look at it properly and he said, Keep it safe.

And I knew he meant keep everything safe, not just the talisman but Tilla and her baby. He meant I must shoulder the care of them wholeheartedly and without fear. In that moment I felt I could.

Suddenly the soldiers came down from the garrison: our friends hurried up the gangplank. Lucius's eyes caught mine for a moment and he smiled a wide, openhearted smile. Then he gestured that Tilla and I should slip away so the soldiers would not see us. But it was too late.

The brutal Minimus, looking at Tilla whose cloak had fallen open, gave a great shout:

Oh my lady, who have you been welcoming between your thighs? One of the randy island goat herds?

The other soldiers jeered at Tilla as they forced us into a little boat that was just leaving to go fishing. They ordered the startled boatman to take us back to the villa. One of the soldiers shouted, as the boat drew away, We'll make sure the Lord and Master in Rome knows about that big belly. The others laughed raucously. Tilla ignored it all: she gazed at Lucius and Dorothea and Zoë as if drawing strength from them.

For a little while, the fishing boat sailed close to the ship carrying our friends away, and we called out wishes for a safe journey, and they called back to us. Then their ship turned towards the mainland. We disembarked at the foot of the rock stairs. We slowly climbed up the long flight to the house with melancholy hearts.

Now, Tilla is reading from her aunt's scroll. Such books are only given to the serious seekers, the Christians said, those like Flavia Domitilla who truly wanted to understand. When they gave the book to Tilla, they hoped to be here a long time and study it with her, explaining the meanings. They said soon she could be baptized and join in their breaking of bread, their private sacred meal. But now they have gone. She has only their gift, the book, which is also a link to Flavia Domitilla and to the whole lost life in Rome.

And I have only the talisman Lucius gave me. It is a piece of tile on which has been scratched the drawing of a basket of bread and a fish.

I hear Tilla murmuring the words she is reading. She somehow absorbed enough Greek in her haphazard childhood to understand the scroll.

I add this after a little hiatus. She stopped her reading, and said to me, Listen to these words, and she read them again for me. The meaning was something like this:

> Mariam went into the hill country, into a town of Judah, and she entered into the house of Zacharias, and she greeted Elizabet. And when Elizabet heard Mariam's greeting, the baby leapt in her womb.

Tilla said, As my own baby leaps.

This makes the book even more precious to her.

A few days before the ides of January.

I awoke this morning to find Tilla pacing the rooms, a blanket drawn around her against the chilly air, holding the book of Loukas, reading, talking, strangely disturbed.

She saw me and said, Listen!

And she read the words of Mariam to the angel:

I am the Lord's handmaid! Let it be with me as you say!

Then she said, Wait, and went ahead in the scroll, searching for other parts she wanted to read to me—how the people of Nazareth, the hometown of Iesous, cast him out and tried to throw him over a cliff, but he kept on preaching. How danger did not stop him from going to Jerusalem. How he accepted his terrible death.

She said, Marina, what is this power that gives Mariam such courage? That makes Iesous go knowingly towards danger over and over again? I am so frightened. Afraid the soldiers will come back, afraid they will tell Domitianus Caesar about this—her swelling belly—and he might order me killed, the child killed. And I am afraid of the birth. I wish I had courage!

Surprised, I said, But you certainly have courage. You have defied the soldiers here more than once. And you challenged Domitianus Caesar.

That was arrogant and foolhardy, said Tilla. Real courage would have been to resist his attentions from the beginning. Real courage was when my aunt and uncle went to him and were angry with him for treating me so. Real courage made Lucius and Zoë and Dorothea sail from Tarracina to Pandateria, and then here to us, even in this season, risking the anger of the sea, and of the guards.

Now she was crying. Suddenly she sat down on the edge of the bed.

I want it, she said decisively, steadying her voice.

I want the peace and calmness and courage that Mariam, Iesous and our Christian friends have. Lucius and Zoë and Dorothea say it is because of what they call the spirit that they came and helped us. I want their spirit, their Iesous. I want to be baptized. I want to break the bread with them.

She sat with her hands on her belly's hillock, and stared at the peeling wall, but she was looking beyond.

Middle of January.

Today it happened again. She stopped moving the shuttle and sat quite still, a hand on her belly, amazed at the sudden tightening. She let me put my hand there to feel how hard it is. Her body is getting ready. Her navel protrudes like a third nipple, and the child, constricted, moves less often. Still sometimes an elbow or a heel pushes up the skin of her belly's dome, curved like a bathhouse roof, and we laugh.

Now we are hurrying to finish the blanket for the baby. The wool is in colours of white and pale green and dark red. I am teaching Tilla a crisscross pattern like those of my people, but a simple one.

Some days after the ides of January. Spring sowing.

Glauca has visited the shrine of the goddess where the island women go, and has prayed and offered sacrifice for Tilla's safe delivery. And also for the germination of the newly sown seed in the fields. She tells stories of women who neglected to make the right offerings. Their babies were too large to be born, or were born backwards. Or were born easily, but the mothers died afterwards of fever. I wish she would tell only stories of good fortune, or keep silent.

Tilla asked me today, Do you know what it is like?

And then she said quickly, I know you have never had a baby yourself, but you have surely seen many births. Perhaps you can tell me something?

She added, I have been present at only one, Flavia Domitilla's last, and I was afraid and could not watch. But I remember she did not scream.

Tilla is right, my body has not been fruitful, but I have seen several births. One or two I have tried to forget and I will never speak of them to her.

I told her of the others, how even the least difficult could not be called easy, but when it was over, the mother's face was full of joy. Like the face of the girl at the first birth I saw, in Britannia.

I was with my mother in the woods, collecting herbs, when a young man found us after a long search. His brother's wife was in a difficult labour. My mother took me with her to the house. She wanted me to help her and watch her work. She wanted me to learn.

It was a day of pelting rain. The baby's father was pressing his forehead against a great tree, imploring the gods for help while the branches thrashed above him.

In the house, the young woman was gripped by pain and terror. It was her first child. She heard the lost voices in the gale outside, and she screamed over and over, afraid for herself and for her baby. I wanted to run away. But I made myself stay there. I tried to be ready if my mother needed my help.

My mother asked the other women to step aside. She sang to the girl and soothed her. She spoke to the Three Mothers, saying: She who binds, She who births, She who gives the breast, hear me now all three: come to this girl. Let her open and release, let her flow like the river water, let her bring the child into the light.

The girl became calmer. She panted as my mother helped her through the pains. At last with a cry of triumph she pushed out from between her thighs a purplish-white lump. It frightened me, until my mother said joyfully, This is a fine baby girl.

My mother called for the man. He was drenched with rain, his dark hair in strings down his cheeks, his clothes heavy with mud. Fear on his face. Then he saw the baby's dark head, damp like his, and her arms and legs uncurling. The new mother gathered her child to the warmth of her breast. The father laughed and cried, the other women murmured in relief. My mother took her special bronze knife and cut the cord, telling me to watch how she tied it in two places.

She finished caring for the girl, the baby, the cord, the afterbirth, and at last, quietly and with deep satisfaction, she gathered up her cloths and elixirs. Later the father would pay her, but this moment was her true recompense.

I hoped she would be with me when my own time came.

About the kalends of February.

Today Tilla has been very tired, and her ankles, so thin before, are swollen. Glauca made an infusion of herbs to restore her.

I brought the drink to her as she lay on a couch. She gave me a smile and a look that warmed my heart, especially when I think how it was between us when we first came to Pontia.

But I feel so helpless. If only Zoë the midwife were still here.

About the fourth day of Parentalia, the Days of the Dead.

It is bitterly cold and windy with a brushing of snow on the terraces.

We stay in one room, huddled near the braziers.

We have nearly finished the blanket for the baby.

Tilla's contractions are stronger and more frequent now.

Next day.

Terrifying news. One of the guards came bursting in. The young one, the boy.

I will not hurt you, he said quickly. I have come to give you a warning.

He told us that the commander has indeed sent word to the emperor Domitianus about Tilla's pregnancy. The emperor has ordered what the guard calls the ultimate penalty for Tilla. Tilla blanched, and spread both hands over her belly.

It was a moment or two before I understood. Then I stepped in front of her, I tried to protect her, I began to plead with him. But he said, No, no, I am here to urge you to escape. None of us relishes following this command, though we know we must. It will not be until after these Days of the Dead are over, after Feralia, the last day.

I asked why he had come to tell us. I feared some kind of trap.

He said, This order sickens me. But the commander intends to carry it out. He does not know I have come here. I can do nothing more to help you, he said, and left.

How, after all these months, can we suddenly rouse ourselves to act? Must we really believe death is so close? Everything seems the same as before: the wind, the crumbling old building, the wintry sea on the rocks below.

Tilla is folding inward, all her energy given to sustaining the life inside her. I shall have to be the stronger one.

I must blow out the lamp, but how can I sleep?

During the Days of the Dead. In the cave of boats.

It has happened, before we could plan our escape. Tilla's labour began towards evening of the day after the soldier came. The pains started slowly at first, as often before. But then they did not stop, they came closer and closer together, through the night. Soon after dawn, her waters broke. She became full of fierce energy, like a mare about to foal seeking the place she needs. Glauca had heard us and was making ready.

Tilla said, Not here. Not in the house, they will find us. A hidden place, somewhere down by the eel pools. Yes, the cave where they put the boats for the winter, she said.

And Glauca, you must stay here, said Tilla, So if the guards come looking for us, you can delay them.

I told Tilla we needed Glauca's knowledge, and Glauca herself was distraught.

But Tilla said to her, If you do not know where I am, and have seen or heard no baby, all the better for you when the guards come to ask. I want only Marina with me.

Now I was truly afraid.

I tried to say again that Glauca had wisdom we needed. Tilla, calm between one pain and the next, answered, You have knowledge too, and so does my body. My aunt used to say, having babies is hard, but the body knows what to do.

Glauca, weeping, gave us garbled instructions and pressed into my hand a bottle containing infusion of verbena, very powerful for safety and to speed the birth, she said. We gathered a few things and came down to this place, down the rock-cut steps, in the grey dawn, in wind and driving rain. Rain as on the day of that first birth I saw. I longed for my mother, for her strength and her gift. The cloaks over our heads were drenched through to our hair, and our legs were tangled in sodden cloth. The rocks were slippery. We held on to the rope stretched between metal posts hammered into the cliff. Down, down, as fast as we could. Tilla had to stop every so often, breathing deep.

Then we came into this cave, out of the wind and wet. The damp air stinks of dead fish, but I do not notice it now. We found this space against the cave wall, among the up-turned boats.

Even in daytime it is dark here. The cave reaches deep into the cliff and curves so you cannot see the cavemouth. I lit a small lamp from the flame in the closed lantern I had carried down. I made a kind of bed against the wall with our damp cloaks.

It was hard to see her suffer. The labour went on and on. Still no child, only the pains, stronger and stronger. I gave Tilla the ver-bena infusion. When I smelled it, I remembered the priests of my people use this herb to see into future time.

Tilla was brave, breathing deep, walking with a bent neck under the low roof until a contraction stopped her. Then she held on to me, breathing, then panting, clasping my hand. And I found I was strong enough to help her through the pains, for hours and hours, many lamps of oil.

At the end the labour was so fierce I thought she could not endure a moment longer, but suddenly her face filled with sur-prise, she said, Now, now, and her knees gave way. I helped her move to the makeshift bed. She squatted against the cave wall, and each time the contraction gripped her, she bore down, grunting, and in between she even laughed.

It's so strong, she said, it takes hold of me.

I crouched in front of her, trying to see by the light of the lamp set on a rock. And there was the top of the baby's head between her legs. I rubbed her with oil so the skin would be supple, and suddenly as she gave a great groan the head emerged. A lit-tle wrinkled face. I cleaned the mouth and nose. Just in time I laid a cloth over my hands. At the next thrust the baby's slippery body, streaked with white vernix, fell right into them: and she shouted in exultation as the body slid out, she leaned down to see the child, she was crying, I was crying, as we looked at the new creature, a boy, and rubbed his chest, and he opened his mouth and wailed.

I lifted him, still attached to the pulsing grey cord, onto Tilla's breast, she held him in her arms. I knew the cord must be cut carefully. In Rome a midwife told me it should never be done with metal, but with a hard crust of bread or a sharpened reed. My mother had her bronze knife with protective designs along the blade. I had not thought to bring anything. But I have my writing box with me, so after a little while I took the knife I trim my reed pens with, and tied and cut the cord as my mother showed me. I covered the baby with a cloth as he lay on Tilla's breast.

The afterbirth came and I took it and went near the opening of the cave—it was late afternoon—and buried it in a sandy place.

When I returned to Tilla, she was smiling, because the baby was seeking her breast. We helped him find the nipple, and he began to suck. My people say that the first milk makes babies strong. Roman doctors and nurses disagree among themselves. Some think it is harmful. Tilla, like her aunt, does what she wants to do.

We stayed here in the cave as night fell. Tilla ate and drank a little. Then she slept. I did not sleep so quickly, with the sea just outside. I remembered the terrible spirit who lived in the sea-caves of my own land and howled darkly in the night. And I could not forget the guards.

Now it is morning. As I write this in the daylight near the cave-mouth, the sea comes and goes on the rocks. So much has happened in our small world inside this cave, both pain and joy. Now I realise again our great danger. We will be killed if the guards find us.

The same day. Evening.

Tilla is sad because there are no garlands to welcome the baby.
He will have no *lustratio* ceremony on the ninth day. He has no
father to give him a name, to hang the lucky *bulla* around his
neck. Poor child, she said, born to a mother in disgrace, from a
man I never want to speak of or remember.

How do you name a child who, far from inheriting his father's
name, must be hidden from his father? His first name she has
already chosen—Lucilius, for Lucius of Tarracina who himself
was named for Loukas. And Flavianus, from her own name, as
his unmarried mother. Lucilius Flavianus Clemens, then, she
said. Clemens after my uncle, who was like a father to me.

And I think that, like many fathers, her uncle might have had
this illegitimate baby taken away and exposed. Perhaps the baby
is safer for being born in exile. Unless the guards find us.

We have been in this cave only a day and a night and this day
now ending. It is as if we know nothing else. How familiar to
me, already, is the sight of Tilla putting the baby across her lap.
She makes sure his dark head, which lolls on the fragile neck,
is supported by her thigh. She undoes her breastband, releas-
ing the full round breast. She takes the baby, cradles him in one
arm, and with her other hand lifts the breast, fingers spread
on either side of the nipple, and she touches the baby's cheek
with the nipple's tip. He turns his head, opens his sweet, small
mouth wide. She leans back against the rocky wall with him,
and I feel a lurch of desire to know what she knows. To feel what
she feels.

(A little later.)

She gave me the baby for a while. I held him. In the shadows,
I stared at the delicacy of his face. He seemed asleep, but then
moved his lips a little and began to whimper. Before he could
cry, I rocked him, and then, with his warm heaviness in my
arms, words came to me, the words my mother sang to me, my

brother, and our little sister. The lullaby I had not been able to remember for Tilla returned to me now. The song of the bird in the tree. The words came from my long-ago land into this time, this place, for this new small being, Lucilius.

Then I remembered the old spells of protection from harm and sickness and dark that my mother used to say over her children. I spoke them over the baby too. And relief started flowing like milk in me, that after all I do not begrudge Tilla this child. I am her sister, he is her baby, and I am glad. And yet because I saw him born, he is also mine.

Day before Feralia.

We had hoped to try and escape in a few days, after giving Tilla time to regain her strength. But since this morning she has been first hot and then chilled. She shakes with fever.

I know the moment has come. If her fever does not get better, she will die. She cannot stay in this damp cave. But if we go back up to the house, the guards will find her and the baby, and kill us all.

Our only chance is to leave the island.

This morning I looked out over the grey, terrible water. I prayed to all the powers I know: Spirits of this island, powers of the sea, rulers of the tides and winds, protect us on this winter sea. Isis Pelagia, mother and healer, cool the fever, let us journey safely. Iesous, help her. Spirits of my ancestors, give me courage now, enter my blood now.

I prayed in my half-forgotten language, although my land is so distant that even the farthest-wandering spirits of my people cannot hear me. I prayed in Latin and in Greek, until I had no more words.

I climbed back up to the rock stairs to the house, told Glauca of the birth and the fever. She quickly made up a phial of medicine against childbed sickness for Tilla. She also gave me a precious amulet of coral to keep the baby safe. She helped me pack a few of my things and Tilla's, and some of the clothes for Lucilius. I took only what I could fit in one chest. There was no time to detach the almost-finished blanket from the loom.

Glauca said, I will send the garden-boy with you, to help you, and Chloë too.

But I said, No, it must be only me and Tilla and the baby. The fewer of us to be noticed, the fewer to eat and travel and survive, the better.

I left Glauca and Philemon with tears trickling in the creases of their old cheeks. What will the guards do to them when they find us no longer there?

Tilla looks so ill.

There are boats in the cave. But I cannot take one out on the sea without help. The only boat I was ever in alone was the one without oars. I decided to look for the man who works in the eel pools, he who smiled at me during the auspices that promised good fortune. We have seen him in his small boat, passing the opening of our cave. I left the chest in the cave and, with my leather bag over my shoulder, I followed the path round the foot of the cliffs, walking on the wet, seaweedy rocks. I found him bending over the largest pool, in the room of Apollo.

I opened the bag, unwrapped my mother's cloth, and showed him the mirror. I grasped it firmly while his fingers traced the incised swirls on its back. Then I turned it over so he saw his weathered face on the reflecting side.

This is yours for ever, I told him, if you help me. Take us in your boat to Tarracina tomorrow, and in secret.

He looked at me, his eyes almost lost in the wrinkles from screwing his face against the sun, and laughed.

What's to stop me grabbing this trinket and hauling you straight off to the guards, as I should? Have you forgotten these pools and the house above belong to the Emperor? And tomorrow is Feralia, the most solemn of the Days of the Dead. Not a day for such enterprises.

He reached to take it from me, and I was shaking and weak. I knew I had failed.

But then I thought of Tilla, and Lucilius at her breast. I thought of the doom in the young guard's voice when he warned us. I quickly snatched the mirror away, surprising the eel man, and put it back in the bag. I said:

If you take it and betray us, the mirror will never give you a moment's good fortune. It has power, it will bring my people to avenge me. My brother will come and strike off your head and hang it at his belt.

I felt, for a moment, as fierce as Boudica. He laughed again, but uneasily now. He looked at my bag as if he could see the mirror shining through the dark leather. He knew it would fetch a high price. This swayed him, Feralia or no.

The seas are still closed, he said. This early spring weather is treacherous. But it may be mild tomorrow and the winds are unusually favourable. I will do it: but only as far as Circeii.

He wanted the mirror in advance. I told him he would not see it again until we were safely ashore on the mainland.

But will he come for us?

Here in this cave, hardly able to make out the letters in this darkness, I write on this our last night on Pontia. I am afraid to leave the island now.

Tilla is sleeping, her hair damp and tangled. Her breaths are fast and shallow. The baby is asleep too, close to her body, her arm curved around him.

The shadows of the night crowd in: this light is a companion, this notebook a friend. So many fears press upon me.

There is the sea to cross. Then, if we reach the shore, where can we go? Will the talisman of Lucius help us? Will we be able to find the Christians? Will they take us in?

I have been looking at the mirror. Would my mother forgive me? Keep it well she said, and give it to your own daughter. But there is no daughter. The mirror is all I have to save us with.

I am losing the last thing that links me to my mother and my land, except the cloth it is wrapped in. There are worn places on the triple-looped handle from the fingers of my mother and her mother and her mother's mother. The sacred animals in the curving designs, the face that appears and disappears, the parts that look like basketwork, all this is workmanship of my ancestors. It carries old magic.

The mirror gives me courage. My people are warriors. Our men go stripped into battle, torcs shining, hair standing up high, spurred on by the scream of the carnax as it summons the ravens of war. The women are close behind, and no one is afraid. They find their courage together. Or so it always used to be.

I will blow out the lamp, thinking of that.

Tomorrow, if the guards do not find us first, we sail at dawn, on the strength of my grandmother's mother's mirror.

Have you built your ship of death, O have you?
O build your ship of death, for you will need it.
—D.H. Lawrence, "The Ship of Death"

I need a mirror of my own to pay my passage; I need a talisman scratched with the password; I need to be ready for the boat.

When I came here, changed my name, and began a new life, I thought I could put everything behind me. I thought what had happened could not touch me any more. But the memory of it is in the body for ever, in muscle and belly and bone. Something like that may be sealed away, calcified, but it is there, and it makes a difference to every day of your life whether you realise it or not. And every now and then, certain things provoke a sudden anguish, like hearing the cry of a newborn baby.

The home for unwed mothers was in a seaside town on the north Devonshire coast. It was a big, mid-Victorian mansion, draughty and chill that winter and early spring, and we were made to work as hard as under-housemaids, scrubbing the floors, beating rugs, and washing the nappies of the babies who were there, for a short while.

In my rare free moments, I used to go down to the seafront and look at the sea. I stood in the cold wind and watched the waves gathering themselves up and breaking, rolling in and out, over the shingle and back again, as they have always done, like a heartbeat or a pulse, and they calmed me.

On the way to or from the sea, or when I was sent on an errand, I sometimes went into the museum if I had a little extra time. It was inside an old rambling house once belonging to a sea-captain, and it was full, as such small museums often are, of a charming hodge-podge of things, displayed in a style old-fashioned even then. The curator was a serious young man who could see from the way I looked at everything that I was really interested. On my second or third visit he kindly waived the small entrance fee. I asked a question about one of the artifacts, the bracelet of Kimmeridge shale, I think, and gradually we struck up an acquaintance; neither of us ever mentioned my pregnancy or difficult situation, but concentrated solely on the past. It was comforting, his indifference to my swelling body under the coat that would no longer button. We rarely looked at each other, but stared through the glass at the exhibits as we talked about them. There were treasures from all the centuries, but I liked the Iron Age things most; especially the scrap of tooled leather, part of a Romano-British shoe that had survived in some waterlogged corner, and the square half-inch of woven cloth in a faintly visible tartan. These remnants of organic material, preserved by some fluke of chemistry, brought closer the lost life of the past.

If I did look towards the curator, it was not usually at his face, but a sort of glance in the direction of his chest, at my eye level, where an embossed metal nametag was pinned to his lapel. So now, thinking about him as I have not done for years, I remember that his name was Robert Hughes.

I wonder if he is still there. Though of course that is most unlikely; it was thirty years ago.

Apart from those small outings, my life was spent at the maternity home. Every so often a girl began her pains and then Mrs White would drive her off to hospital and return without her. I wondered what it was like for the girl to be left there to go through this enormous, unimaginable thing alone. When girls came back with their babies, we did not dare to ask about the birth. Some were silent, withdrawn into themselves. A few showed bravado, saying, "Nothing to it, really." Every baby soon disappeared, and not long afterwards the mother left as well.

At twenty-two I was the oldest mother-to-be there. Before my baby came, one of the younger girls asked, "Will you keep it, then? You're old enough to go off on your own and do what you want."

I did not know how to explain that in my mother's eyes I was still young, and in my own as well; I felt nowhere near old enough to do whatever I wanted to do. And what would that be, anyway? The baby, although I had grown accustomed to its presence within me, still seemed unreal and unimaginable. More than anything I wanted to be back on the right path, to be acceptable again.

Then one morning when I was scrubbing the floor there was a strange leakage, a splash, and it was my turn to be taken to hospital, bumping along in the home's old van, with the labour pains beginning. Hardly able to speak for fear, I croaked out to Mrs White, "Will it hurt very much?"

"Oh yes, I expect so," she answered briskly, "But you should have thought of that before."

And of course it did hurt very much, and I was ignorant and terrified. The nurses and the doctor made me lie flat on my back, spreadeagled, though I wanted to sit up. Yet near the end, my body took over with unstoppable muscular force, not in time with their officious cries of "Push! Push!" but to its own rhythm; and at last I met the unknown, yet known, companion of all those months. A baby. My baby; a dark-haired girl. They took her away to clean and dress her, and I kept saying, "Give her back to me, give her back," until they laid her in my arms.

Everything changed then. She was so beautiful with her amazing head of black hair. She moved that head against me, searching, and I put her to my breast, where she attached herself with easy instinct and sucked as if never to let me go. I held her close.

Was it cruel to allow us to fall in love with our babies and then to take them away? Would it have been better or worse if I had seen her only briefly and then lost her for ever, as happened to some birth mothers elsewhere? I cannot tell. At least I know I gave her my milk and my love for the first six weeks. Once she was gone, that love became unendurable. I could only survive by suppressing it completely.

I longed to keep my baby. It would be selfish, they said. What kind of life could she have, illegitimate, poor, with a mother struggling from day to day? No landlord would accept you, no employer would take you on with an infant. And all the time there is a nice family waiting to give her a good home, and the security she could never have with you.

But she would have love, I thought, the love of her own mother, and we would be together. My body was committed now to motherhood. My milk came in, and dampened my bra when I heard her cry; my arms shaped themselves around the weight of her. I had studied her eyes, and her mouth, and her hands with long fingers like her father's, her lovely skin. I knew her, from dark head to tiny toe. And she was learning to know me. She began to turn towards my voice, and follow me across a room with her eyes.

"Don't get too attached," said Mrs White. "Very soon she will be gone for ever."

For ever. Here in America they spell it as one word: forever. This seems all wrong, this pushing the words together, rushing that which never ends. *For ever*, two separate words, with the glottal stop between them slowing everything down, a phrase with long melancholy vowels and the echo of "ever" lingering on the ear, is more evocative of eternity.

I heard them say she would be gone for ever, but I could not understand what it really meant. Even as I agreed to relinquish my baby, I somehow thought it was only for a while.

Everyone told me, over and over, that adoption was for the best.

"If you really love your baby, you will give her up," they said. In confusion and misery I signed the papers.

Over the years, these buried memories had faded like dreams, or so I thought; but now, as I return to what happened, suddenly the intervening years all fall away. The pain is visceral, as if still new.

In Marina's notebook there is a large gap in time after she tells of waiting for the boat to take them away from Ponza. She did not write in the notebook again until fourteen years later. But then when she took it up once more, and began to remember, perhaps those fourteen years evaporated, and for her too the past became as real as the present.

So many years have gone by since I wrote in this book. It is from another time, another place: a different life. I put it away after I left Pontia. I was busy enough living.

Now something has happened that has made me take out the book again, and read it, and write in it once more.

Lucilius has disappeared. He is fourteen years old now, a young man, restless as young men are. He has gone off with a band of marauders who wreak havoc and think themselves so brave. He galloped away after the hay was gathered in. I do not know where, or for how long. His last angry words are burned into my mind.

In this anxiety, I have returned to the past. I have read over and over these old pages, with their smell of the salt air of Pontia. Here I wrote of the beginning of his life fourteen years ago. Here are the threats and the dangers. Here is the joy of his birth. And here are the last words I wrote, as we waited for the boat to take us away.

After we left Pontia, everything was different. The habit of writing in this book was no longer part of my life. And the book reminded me of my sorrow.

Now, however, I should complete this account. Perhaps in
returning to time gone by, I can escape the present with its tor-
menting thoughts.

This book, begun in the loneliness of exile to Pontia, became
something I did not expect: the story of Tilla and how I grew to
know and love her. And I must tell the end of that story. I must
tell the most difficult part.

The boatman did not fail us. I sat in his boat as it rode over the
waves, its movement sickening me as always. I was holding the
baby who was crying and crying, with Pontia growing smaller
and smaller behind. Then, just the sea, until in front of us the
mainland of Italy finally appeared and gradually became clearer
and closer.

But that is not the difficult part.

In the cave on Pontia, as I tried to plan our escape, I thought
that I would be the strong one, stronger than Tilla. This was an
illusion.

We waited. At last the darkness lifted and the delicate pink
came into the sky.

We stepped out onto the rock in front of the cave, Tilla holding the baby. She was shivering with fever and the chilly morning air.

The sea was quiet, but still dangerous. I was afraid that the boat
would not come, and afraid that it would. The baby mewed a little. Tilla's breasts were filling with real milk now. She planned to
feed him on the journey.

Then the boat appeared from behind the cliff. It was very small.
The eel pool man and another boatman in their broad-brimmed
hats jumped out and pulled it as close to the rocks as they could.
We waded towards it, feet chilled, clothes dragging in the cold
water. When I was aboard with our baggage, Tilla passed me
the baby, and climbed in herself. Just as she sat down I saw the
soldiers on the clifftop, running back and forth, looking for
the stairs cut in the rock, shouting at us to stop. But both men
started rowing with all their strength. The boat moved as the

soldiers began climbing down and the commander waved his sword. Fear pierced my heart, prickled my scalp, I held the baby tight, the men rowed, but we were still in shallow water. The soldiers would reach us before we could get away. Then Tilla stood up, and suddenly stepped right out of the rocking boat, lifting her skirt as it caught for a moment on the wood, falling to her knees in the water as the boat lurched away from her.

A space of sea opened up between her and the boat, I tried to make the men stop rowing, I begged Tilla to come back, I shouted at her so loudly the baby began to cry hard. Tilla scrambled to her feet and called out, Go, take him, go quickly!

She stood there, water up to her thighs, her yellow tunic tight against her swollen breasts, two damp patches spreading where the new milk flowed. She waved us away with arms that had held the baby almost every moment since his birth.

The men pulled on the oars and hoisted the sail, the boat was moving fast through the sea now, and there stood Tilla in the shallows, more and more distant. The guards had found a path down the cliff. Just as we began to round the point they reached her. Their boots kicked up the water, the white foam bright in the sun. I saw the glint of metal, her body falling. And then we rounded the headland and it blocked everything out.

The wind, bitter cold, filled the sail: the boat moved towards the horizon, leaving Pontia behind, leaving Tilla under the soldiers' swords.

I sat rigid. Only long afterwards did I realise that, although I felt sickness, I had no fear of the sea at all on that journey. There was only the horror of what had happened to Tilla.

The baby wailed more and more desperately. He nuzzled against my breast, seeking what I could not give. Now I would need to find a wet nurse as soon as we reached land. One of the boatmen had vinegar water, and I offered him some, but it only made him cry more.

He screamed fiercely, as if he knew I had left his mother there to die.

I should have stepped out of the boat myself, I should have given her the baby and stepped out and let the boat take them away. I should have been the one under the swords. I cursed myself for my slowness, my cowardice, for letting her once again do the reckless thing, this time not dragging me with her into exile, but setting me free instead. And yet I could not help being glad I was free, sailing to safety, and Lucilius safe with me.

The island disappeared behind us and the white specks catching the sun on the coast ahead became larger and larger until I could see they were buildings. And then the men were tying up in the harbour of Circeii, and hurrying me and my baggage and the baby off the boat.

Now, the mirror, demanded the eel pool man. He was angry because the soldiers had seen us, and perhaps recognized him. There was danger for him in returning to Pontia. Awkwardly, because of the baby, I reached into my bag, lifted the bundle out, and undid the cloth. I put the mirror into his net-scarred and lobster-torn hands. He sat suddenly on a coil of rope as if the mirror's weight pulled him down. I left him there turning it over and over.

I wrapped Lucilius in the cloth my mother wove.

There I stood alone on the quay with the baby in my arms and the boxes at my feet. There were many buildings, and many people even though it was winter. There was jostling, confusion, shouting. I did not know what to do, where to go. The baby was exhausted from crying. Towards the end of the boat journey, he had slept, whimpered, woken and cried again, more weakly every time. Now I was his false mother. And I did not have the nourishment his real mother could give.

Tilla and I had hoped to find Lucius and the other Christians in Tarracina. But I was in Circeii, under the mountain of Circe. Where could I find Christians in this town? They were usually found in the part of a town where the craftsmen and small shops are. I hired one of the ragamuffins at the quay and asked him to carry the boxes to such a district. He led me to a small piazza with a fountain and benches nearby. The streets radiating from it were full of workshops—silversmiths, shoemakers, weavers. Some were closed for Feralia. I paid the boy and sat there with the baby and the baggage. People came to the fountain to drink or to fill a water-jug and I watched them. After a while one woman asked me kindly about the baby and I decided to take a risk. I showed her the talisman of the bread and fish.

She said, I know some people who use that sign. She led me to the house of a Jewish Christian woman, Sara. Sara had a friend with a new baby. This woman was willing to feed Lucilius for a day or two. And they helped me find a wagon driver who would take us along the coast to Tarracina.

A few days later we came to Tarracina with the mountain of Neptune rising high above it, the enormous temple at the summit. In the town, after a weary search, I found Lucius's sister in her shop. He was away traveling. His sister led me to Dorothea and Zoë.

There was joy at our meeting, and delight over the baby Lucilius. But there was great sadness as I told them what had happened to Tilla.

We will never let her name be forgotten, they said. She is one of us, even if there was no time for her to be baptized. Her courage will always be praised and remembered among the Christians of Tarracina.

It is the next day, Lucilius is still gone, and to keep my hand and my mind busy I continue this account.

Dorothea took us in. She found a wet nurse, Fabia, a woman of Tarracina whose own baby had just died. Lucilius was still not eight days old, fragile from all that he had already suffered. On his eighth day, she gave him the gift of a *bulla* to wear around his neck. It was not of gold, as it would have been were he a legitimate son of the Flavian house, but of leather. Among the charms in it to keep him safe were a tiny plaque of silver with the Christian fish sign, and the piece of coral Glauca had given me for him. To celebrate his naming and his survival of the first eight days, Dorothea prepared a small dinner and invited Zoë and other friends. I almost wept with gratitude for this welcome.

Dorothea knew I did not want to be a burden on her scant resources, and arranged for me to work. I wrote letters and drew up contracts for her and for other Christians. Sometimes I helped people read. They wanted to study for themselves the letters of Paulos and the memoirs of the apostles that they heard in the meetings. They also wanted me to make copies of these writings.

I began thinking about the idea I had on Pontia, that the Christians, who used books often in their teaching, might find it more convenient if the books were notebooks and not scrolls. In Rome many people such as accountants and merchants had begun using notebooks for their records instead of wax tablets. Quintilian often used notebooks of parchment or papyrus. Some booksellers were selling even the works of great writers in parchment pages.

One morning, when Dorothea brought me a scroll I was to copy, I asked her if she remembered my notebook, this very one, which she seen me use on Pontia. I brought it to her and showed her how it is easier to manage a notebook like this than a scroll. To find a particular passage while teaching is simple. And a notebook is much more compact when traveling.

She said, But these writings of our teachers are precious to us. Surely they should be in a scroll like other important writings?

I replied, Perhaps. But did not Iesous and his followers travel long distances, and Paulos and Loukas too? Did they not live simply, as working men who carried little on their journeys?

It was agreed that I would copy the scroll onto another scroll, as requested, and also into a notebook. It was a collection of the letters of Paulos. I showed both copies to the man who had ordered the work. He preferred the notebook. Then many more commissions followed from the other Christians. I made copies of their writings in notebooks of papyrus and sometimes parchment.

Everyone scrupulously paid me with food, clothing, or money. Thus I supported myself, and the baby Lucilius, and paid his nurse, Fabia. I was terrified when Lucilius caught fevers and sicknesses, and once he was so ill we thought he would die. But he lived. He was a beautiful baby. Dorothea used to say, How lucky it is that you came to us. We have a skilled scribe just when we needed one. And I have a new grandson! She never saw her own grandchildren: her sons kept them away because she was a Christian.

She was so kind to me. They were all kind. They were patient with my enduring sadness. I wept often for Tilla, and they comforted me.

When I saw Lucius again, for the first time since he and Dorothea and Zoë sailed away from the Pontia harbour, my heart lifted. I was drawn to him, although I knew it was unwise. For I was beginning to grow restless, after the first shock and grief over Tilla had passed. The Christians treated me like a friend. I knew they hoped I would eventually become one of them. But I did not truly belong there.

One morning in the marketplace, in early summer, I noticed a stall I had never seen before. It was laden with woolen cloaks and blankets in crisscross stripes of many colours, the cloth they make only in Britannia. I was looking, and thinking of my mother, when out of the shadow of the awning I heard a thin voice: Fine British shawls! There was an old woman crouching on a stool. I could hear in the way she spoke Latin that she came from my own land.

I said, These shawls remind me of home.

She stood up then and came out into the sun. She had a wisp of faded, once-red hair pinned on her head in a meager coil. Her face was all creases. The mark on her scrawny wrist showed she was not of my people, but from a place nearby. She asked in Latin why I was in Tarracina. Stumbling, I replied in my language, our language. She answered, stumbling even more than I did. She had forgotten more of the words. She told me how, long ago, there came to her town, called Vindocladia or White Walls, a merchant from Tarracina selling pottery and fish sauce. She loved his goods, and him too. She told me just what she loved him for, cackling, her toothless mouth wide. She went to Italy with him. They had children, the years passed, and they never made the long journey back to her home. Her husband settled in Tarracina and sold British goods brought to him through a network of other merchants. Her children had children of their own. They delight her, but all this time she has missed her own country more and more. She always thought she would go back one day. Now she is old, and often ill.

I can never return, she told me, wiping away the water spilling from her wet eyes. The skin, dragged by her bony knuckle, moved loosely over her cheekbone.

She said, Perhaps when I reach the land of the dead I will see those hills again. Perhaps I will be able to see the living, to look at my sisters, and their children and grandchildren. And find my mother, so long dead herself.

All the years had not worn away her desire. It was still as sharp as the thin metal point of a pen. She had spent her whole life longing to be in another place.

A few days have passed since I wrote. Still no sign of Lucilius, nor word of him.

On Pontia, the desire to return to my own country had been awakened when I spoke of my childhood with Tilla. In Tarracina this desire grew stronger. I began to dream of going back. Yet the binding words of Broccomagus forbade it. And even if there were no spell against me, I could never pay for the journey.

I was grateful for Dorothea's generosity, but I knew I could not stay with her much longer. I had rested on her kindness long enough.

I could not go back to Rome with Lucilius as long as that madman was still on the Palatine. Even if I could find relatives and friends of Flavia Domitilla who wanted to help us, it was too dangerous. And Tarracina itself was not safe from the emperor's far-reaching power: he had a summer residence there.

Of course I did not know that a few months later Domitianus would be dead.

Lucilius was my charge now, mine to keep safe. But I could not see how best to do that.

I admired the Christians. I liked the way they gave without reserve. However, that summer there was trouble among them. Some thought Christians could have friendships even with those who did not share the same beliefs. Lucius and Dorothea and Zoë were among this group. Even they, however, disapproved of marriage with those outside the fold.

Others, one Felix the most vocal, maintained Christians should hold themselves apart. The kingdom of God is not of this world. Felix criticized Lucius for his friendships with outsiders. Then he began to say Dorothea should not have me in her house any longer, unless I agreed to take instruction.

Perhaps Tilla would have wanted Lucilius to grow up among Christians and become one of their number. But she was gone. I had to do what I believed best for him and for me. I did not want Christian instruction. I still belonged to my own land with its green and glistening gods. I belonged to the spirits of that place, and to the ancestors who lived in those hills and valleys before us.

Go, book, and greet for me all the beloved places,
thus I'll come as close as possible to walking in them myself.
—Ovid, *Tristia ex Ponto*

After the baby, my mother thought it would all be as if nothing had ever happened, and I would go on to my planned success, and she would be able to take pride in me. But I could not forgive her for making me surrender my daughter. I was even less able to forgive myself.

There was no question of finishing the doctorate; I had missed so much time, but more than that, I had become a different person. I could not remain at home with my mother. Nor could I stay anywhere near where the baby had been born; I knew I would gaze at every little girl I saw, and wonder if she were mine. I had been told the family who adopted her lived not far away; I did not trust myself not to seek her out. I had to make some sort of plan, but I was unable to concentrate on anything.

In the end I fled to America, which I could enter freely because the father I never knew had bequeathed me, if little else, American citizenship. I wanted a new beginning. In England my baby had been torn away from me; if she and I could not have a life there together, then I would take my fractured self away from the place that broke us apart. I arrived under the name on my birth certificate, but as soon as possible I legally changed my first name and I became Aubrey. I did not believe then that I would ever want to be found. I could not have imagined how bitterly I would come to regret this self-erasure.

Now, as I remember in these pages everything that happened, all that I tried for so long to forget, I begin to wonder about smaller questions as well as the large, impossible ones. Through international directory inquiries, I learned that the little museum I used to linger in while pregnant is still there. I called, or rather I should say, I rang them up; and I was told that the curator Robert Hughes had moved on years ago, and was now in charge of a museum in Dorset.

The Dorset coast is where Marina, according to the clues she gives us, comes from. I went to that coast when I was in England working on her manuscript. I have been inside the scooped-out circle of Lulworth Cove; I have climbed high above the sea and stood on the sweeping slopes of Bindon Hill, traced the faint swells under the grass of ancient ditches and ramparts. It seemed like a giant round snail shell. I breathed the sweet grassy aroma and saw the wildflowers Marina may have known—milkwort, vetch, buttercup, and ling. Folk legend says the attacking Roman armies can still be heard and even seen, marching over the hills. The ancient British tried to defend themselves by enclosing a huge area of the hilltop with dykes and earthworks. Bindon Hill could be the high place Marina speaks of, or she could have meant nearby Flowers Barrow, also once a British hill fort.

Whether Lulworth, or nearby Mupe Bay, both semi-circular, or some other bay was the particular one she calls "our cove," the "cove of the moon," is not clear. But that piece of coast is where she was born and lived as a small girl, and heard the sound of the sea as it sucks back from the pebbles, and crashes on the rocks. She might have helped gather the leather-like brown straps of seaweed to fertilize the land. Somewhere on these high windy cliffs she saw the dolphins and found her name as a woman; and in the cliff-face of one of those bays, where samphire and pink thrift grow from the chalk, she hid the stone with her newly written name in Latin.

I have been wondering what I will do with this book. And I think I might send it to Robert Hughes, who knew me when the baby was still nested inside my body. I remember feeling he was a trustworthy man. And in sending it to the museum in Dorset where he is now, I would be sending Marina's story home.

The hazel nuts are ripening. Still Lucilius has not returned, and no one has heard anything of him. It is normal for a young man, I know. He is at the age where he cannot be hobbled like a pony to a stake. But he left in anger.

He said words I cannot forget: You are not my mother. I have no mother, no father. I belong nowhere. What does it matter where I go or what happens to me?

He hates the Romans and all they have done and are still doing to us. He hates the Roman blood in his own veins.

When he was a baby, that late spring and early summer in Tarracina, as I wondered whether to stay with the Christians, or whether to leave them, and where to go, he with his fat cheeks and his laughter was the delight of my life.

One day during that time I was with my friend Brica, the old British woman at the market. There came a merchant Corin from Britannia who sometimes brought goods for her to sell. He knew her part of the land and her sisters and their children. He and the old woman spoke together, naming one person and then another, there under the Italian sun evoking the places and people she had left behind long ago. He did not know my village but he sometimes went to the town of Durnovaria, a morning's ride away from it.

Then he asked Brica, Here in Tarracina, do you know any of the followers of Chrestus or Christus?

She said, Marina knows those people. And he went with me to meet them.

He spoke at their gathering as follows:

I come from a very distant country, a chilly, misty place. My people have many gods, and now the Romans think to tame our gods to their own ends. And with the Romans, and the merchants from distant lands, come new gods and new philosophies. We have word of Mithras and of Isis and of this Way of Christus. Some of my people would like to know more about these things. Can you teach me?

Felix stood up suddenly, and he said: Surely this is a message for us from the Spirit. This man is like the man from Macedonia that Paulos saw in his dream. We are called to go ourselves to Britannia, my brothers and sisters.

He turned to the British merchant.

Will you escort us and guide us in your land? he asked.

Corin was taken by surprise but responded graciously.

I would be honoured to do so, he said.

Then, cried Felix, so be it! The time is short, the end of days is near. We must make haste. Who will come with me?

The Christians spoke among themselves, many alarmed at the idea of this sudden uprooting, but some eager for adventure. The merchant and I went back to old Brica in the market to see if she wanted to travel with them, to go home at last.

Brica shook her head sadly.

It is too late, she said. I am too old for the journey. I can barely bring these dry sticks of bones to the market every day.

She peered into my face with her watery blue eyes, and gripped my hand hard:

You must go, Marina. You must take this chance or there might never be another. You will grow old and die here in this foreign land, far from your ancestors. You must find the courage.

But I did not know how.

I continue this account as the leaves change their colours.

Felix and some others began to make preparations to go to Britannia. Even if I wanted to join them, I doubted Felix would allow it. And Lucilius still needed his nurse, Fabia.

I could not ask her to leave her home and friends and go to a strange distant place. She was a widow with no surviving children, but she was a free woman, not my slave.

Then I was afraid of what I would find in my homeland after so much time. Were my parents still alive? Were our houses still there, and the pigs, the flocks of sheep? The horses, the fields, the stronghold up on the cliff?

Broccomagus had power to bind his curse into the roots, the trees, the cliffs, the sea, so the poison against me was everywhere, in sap and stone and water, even in the drops of rain. All the gods of that place, the stag-horned lord and the three mothers and the sea powers, all were marshaled against my return.

One day I told Zoë about the word of death that the druid had laid upon me. I told her how it meant anyone could kill me with impunity, and the land and sea themselves were turned against

me. How he had cried in his voice of iron, Death if you set foot
on this shore again.

Zoë said, I do not know your land. I do not know its demons.
But you must not even speak of them: for the power of Iesous
is stronger. If you trust in it, no harm will come to you. I knew
when I first saw you on Pontia that you were meant to go back to
your land. And Lucius said so too.

Lucius was part of what held me in Tarracina. When I looked at
his strong body, at his eyes, his smile, I could not help hoping he
might think of taking a non-Christian wife, one day. But I knew
even Zoë and Dorothea did not believe he should do that. He
would be torn between his chosen way of life and a woman.

If little Lucilius survived the perils of the journey and reached
my land, he would be far from the taint of Tilla's exile and disgrace, far from the tyrant who wanted to kill him.

I was the mother of Lucilius now. Mothers learn from their own
mothers. If my mother was still alive, I wanted her to help me.
I needed her voice. I needed the voices of other women, alive
and dead, who could show me how to rear him in the ways of
my people.

Perhaps I did not think carefully enough. I did not consider
that returning to the place of my own ancestors would mean
taking him away from his. I only knew that until I went back
I was somehow unfinished, like the blanket Tilla and I left on
the loom.

Another day with no word.

At that time in Tarracina I thought so often of Tilla, my sister,
my friend. She chose to step out of that boat. I saw it: she let go
of the baby she loved, for his safety's sake, and she let go of her
own life lightly.

Surely I could find the courage to travel back to Britannia and
look for my mother. I could find the courage to face whatever
darkness or mystery waited for me there.

First I needed to speak with Lucius. Nothing had been said between us. I waited for him after one of their meetings. He came out of the house and we sat on a wall in a patch of shade cast by an olive tree.

I asked him very simply, Do you think I should go back to Britannia, if Felix will take me?

I wanted him to say Yes. I wanted him to say No.

He looked at me, and under his gaze I almost forgot everything, I almost begged him not to let me leave. He said, I told you on Pontia that you should go back some day. This seems the right time. But only you can be sure.

I was silent, and so was he. Then I felt him gathering himself to say words that must be said, words he knew would give pain. I believe they pained him too.

Marina, if you have any hope that we might enter into a bond closer than friendship, relinquish it now.

He stooped and picked up a twig that had fallen from the tree.

He said he wished it were possible. But he had been called to spread word of the Kingdom, called to a life of travel and hardship. He could not take a woman into the dangers of such a life, he said, especially one who did not share his belief. Most especially one who had a child.

We did not look at each other as he spoke. I felt the warmth of his body beside me. I stared down at his fingers playing with the twig, and I saw they were shaking.

Marina, he said, it is better for us both if you go away.

I never saw him so sad, and so serious. He had given me my answer.

But to go away was not so easy.

My heart and my body were hungry for life with a man. Perhaps if I stayed I could overcome his hesitations. Or become Christian one day.

Yet I also knew I would never rest until I had reached my own land and tried to find my own people.

Felix did not welcome me as one of the travelers. He said, You do not share our beliefs, you wish simply for protection. And how can you pay for your passage? It is not possible.

At that moment, when he said, It is not possible, I suddenly knew it must be. I must return.

I told Felix: Remember I have skill in writing and copying. Surely you need to take many copies of your writings with you? And in notebooks, as they are so much easier to travel with than scrolls? You need me to make more copies. And also to write letters the travelers can send back to their friends and families. It will be worth your while to pay for my journey.

I will think about this, he answered, and walked away.

Then a Christian man intending to travel with the group lost his wife in childbirth. The baby survived. The father wanted more than ever to depart, but would not leave his baby, and the baby needed a wet nurse. So Felix agreed I could join the travelers as a scribe and copyist, if the nurse Fabia came too and fed the new baby as well as Lucilius. The father was a wealthy man. Fabia was willing, and she loved Lucilius. She assured me she would have milk enough for both children.

And so it was settled at last. All the obstacles had fallen away.

Zoë said, The Spirit of Iesous is guiding these events.

I told her I was thankful to that Spirit. And I went to the temple of Isis and I offered her a vow, one I would fulfil if Lucilius and I safely reached Britannia.

Then I walked down to the harbour and looked at the ships. Not all of our journey would be by sea, Corin had told us. Some would be by river and over land. But it would begin on the sea, and end on it, for my country lay far beyond oceans.

My heart constricted in terror as I saw the network of rigging and the spiky masts of the ships. Their sails looked thin against the storm winds, and their hulls seemed like little baskets.

But when I looked below me into the water, I saw many small jellyfish swimming between the wharf supports, opening, closing, each one like a flower. I watched and they gradually brought me a little peace. Their opening and closing, in and out, was like breathing deeply, at rest.

And did those feet, in ancient time,
Walk upon England's mountains green?
—William Blake, from Preface to *Milton A Poem*

Absent clear physical vestiges of Christianity in Britain in the first and second centuries, there are many evocative legends. There is the story that Joseph of Arimathea was a tin merchant and went to Britain with the boy Jesus; even that Jesus showed Joseph how to mine tin in Cornwall. There was the tradition that after Joseph gave up his own tomb for the burial of Jesus, he sailed back to Britain, settled in Glastonbury, and built a wattle church there. When he thrust his staff into the West Country earth, it took root and lived ever after as the Glastonbury Thorn; or perhaps the Thorn grew from a piece of the Crown of Thorns. But the most precious object Joseph carried to Glastonbury was the cup Jesus used at the Last Supper, the Holy Grail.

Gildas, the monk who wrote in the early 500s of the *excidio* or ruin of his country, Britain, says that the "beams of light" from "Christ, the true Sun" came to "these islands stiff with frost" at the end of the reign of Tiberius, who died only a few years after Jesus himself. These rays, Gildas adds, "were received with lukewarm minds by the inhabitants." Gildas acknowledged the lack of historical accounts; he said he would describe the evils Britain suffered under the Roman emperors without "the writings and records of my own country, which (if there ever were any of them) have been consumed in the fires of the enemy, or have accompanied my exiled countrymen into distant lands."

The church father Tertullian, writing around 200 AD in Rome or Carthage, claimed Christianity had reached even the furthest haunts of the Britons, the distant edge of the earth as it would have seemed to him.

British Christianity moves from myth towards history with the deaths of Britain's first known martyrs: Alban, Aaron, Julius, and other men and women whose names are lost. They may have died in the persecution of Christians under Diocletian, around 300, or perhaps years earlier in a different persecution. Aaron and Julis probably died in Caerleon, and Alban at the place later called after him. Alban was not yet a Christian when he hid a fleeing priest in his house, but he was moved by the man's faith, learned it from him, and adopted it. Finally he wrapped himself in the fugitive's long cloak and gave himself up in his stead. At his martyrdom there were miracles; he was given power over the waters, he dried up a river, and he called forth a spring.

Constantine established the Peace of the Church in 313, and Christians were safe. The following year, church leaders gathered for a synod in Arles. Three bishops from Britain attended; but of the British Christian life they represented, we have few remaining material fragments. There are floor mosaics, including a portrait of Christ; there are Christian symbols engraved on silver bowls, or carved in lead tanks used for footwashing or baptism. There are a few buried hoards of precious objects, including tableware decorated with the monogram cross, and spoons bearing the Christian phrase "*vivas in deo*," may you live in God.

Then there are the stories of Patrick, born in fifth-century Britain and taken to Ireland by raiders; David, known as The Water Man because in his austere rule he and his monks drank only water; Columcille, the traveler who left Ireland after a dispute over possession of a book, and went to Iona, where he and his monks settled in a place chosen because from it they could no longer see the beloved Irish shore and be tormented by homesickness. They and many others chose to be *peregrini*, to be foreigners and outsiders, to live as pilgrims for God.

Gildas gives a glimpse of the "diabolical idols" of pre-Christian beliefs in his country Britain: "We still see some mouldering away within or without the deserted temples, with stiff and deformed features as was customary." Only a very few have survived to our day, sculptures of deities like the three mothers and Cernunnos and others, many of whose names are not known. Of the druids, very little is known beyond what the classical writers wrote. Of the Romans, something is left to us, though little compared to what the Venerable Bede of Jarrow described around 730, Roman cities, forts, bridges and paved roads still to be seen across the land; the Saxons called them "the work of giants."

There are still places in Britain where the layers of the past are visible, if faintly, back to the Romans and even beyond. The ancient church at Daglingworth in the Cotswolds contains Saxon carvings of Peter and Christ that were found hidden in a pillar, and one of its windows was carved out of a Roman stone. Centuries before that, someone incised words on the stone, still just visible, recording the vow one Junia made to the *genius loci*. The church builders must have found the stone in the ruins of a nearby Romano-British temple or shrine.

There are countless villages and towns like this, where people have been born, lived, and died for millennia on the slopes of the same hill or the banks of the same river; where cars follow pathways once grooved by medieval cartwheels, walked by Iron Age farmers. These layers of history nourish us who grow up there, nourished me even when I was unaware of them. But much has disappeared over the centuries, sometimes gradually through the erosion of time, sometimes in sudden swathes of ruin.

If other Christian missionaries or merchants, besides Marina's companions, arrived in Britain at the end of the first century, as they may well have done, nothing recognizable of their presence remains. Their stories are lost to us now.

⌐‑‑‑‑‑‑‑⌐

We left Tarracina in June, with Lucilius a baby who could not yet sit up. First we sailed north along the coast to Ostia, where we found a large ship bound for Narbo. Five days on that ship, sailing against the wind, sleeping on deck, cooking in the hearth when the crew permitted. The ship always rolling and bucking on the sea. From Narbo a long journey partly in wagons, partly

by river, until we reached the River Garumna. Then an endless journey across Gallia by riverboat to Burdigala on the oppo-
site coast.

We stayed in Burdigala for a while. The river ends there in a
wide marshy expanse, and flows into the open ocean, on which
we were to sail. We all felt a great fear of venturing into those
stormy unpredictable waters. But this was our destined route.

The ships hugged the coast as closely as possible, while trying
to avoid the rocks. We crept slowly northward, skirting many
islands. We anchored at the harbours where the merchants
sold wine and oil and other goods we had brought from Italia. We took on cargoes of pottery and locally made fish sauce.
We slept on the deckboards, or at filthy harbour taverns full of
mosquitoes and fleas. I was anxious for the health of Lucilius.
But Fabia was well. The father of the younger baby made sure
the Christians gave her plenty of good food, and she did not
even suffer as I did from seasickness. Lucilius grew fat and
strong on her milk. He loved to be held where he could watch
the seagulls swooping and crying around the ship, hoping
for scraps.

We went from one rickety ship to the next. We spent days in
harbour waiting for winds to turn or storms to die down. There
were bad omens, and good omens. Underneath it all was my fear
of what would happen when I returned to my country, mixed
with my longing to return.

At last we safely rounded the dangerous rocky headland called
the End of the Earth, and entered the Britannic Ocean. We
anchored in a harbour on the north shore of Gallia and waited
for the tide to turn. Then we began the final and most difficult
part of the journey, with strong tides bearing us swiftly towards
the British coast. The winds were fierce and the waters wild.
The sickness overwhelmed me, and the terror of the druid's
curse, until I wished to die.

Then a miraculous wonder occurred: three dolphins came right
up close to the ship, and stitched in and out of the sea alongside

us, escorting us to landfall. We had seen dolphins now and then
in our journey, but these swam closer than any others. As they
rolled in the sea alongside the ship they looked at us with infi-
nite knowedge. I knew they were my own dolphins, the three
that saluted me on my naming day. The same three that played
alongside my oarless boat before Cosmas fished me up out of
the water. They came as messengers from the powers of the deep
to tell me I should not be afraid. But the Christians thought the
dolphins were a sign from their god.

At last the ship drew close to the coast. First I saw the white-
ness of the shore in the distance. Then the rocky cliffs, the cliffs
of my own place, but that was not our destination. We passed
them until the landscape became flatter, and green, and there
was an opening into a wide harbour. The boat slipped in, and
then we were on a stretch of water all enclosed by land. Here it
was calm at last. The boat bumped against the stone quay and
then was tied up firmly, and we disembarked.

I had never been to this port as a child but I knew it was about a
day's ride from our village.

I had forgotten the greenness of my land. And the deep undergrowth of bushes, trees, and wild flowers. The dark woods
standing full of mystery. Full of the powers ready to do
me harm.

We stayed at the harbour for a night. I went to the temple of
Isis to fulfil the vow I had made so long before in Tarracina. I
sold two gold bracelets of Tilla's to a smith and he melted them
down and made a tiny golden boat. I dedicated it to the goddess
in thanksgiving for a safe journey. And I prayed for her protection against the curse of Broccomagus.

The next morning the merchant Corin engaged wagons. The
group of Christians, with Fabia, Lucilius, and I, traveled to Vindocladia, the place of white walls. This was Corin's home and
had also been the home of Brica from the Tarracina market.
Here the Christians hoped to find lodging and work, as well as
people receptive to their teaching.

We rode in the wagons through air full of fine mist, and a little rain. It was the time of the harvest, so the people needed dry weather, but the rain fell refreshing and welcome on my face. It was the soft rain I had longed for so often in the heat of Pontia.

The crops stood in the fields full and ready. The rain stopped and we saw people cutting down the tall stalks with sickles, and separating grain from chaff. I saw children gathering the grain in baskets, as I used to. The air was soft and mild upon my skin. I knew the scent of it. Yet still no harm came to me from the curse of Broccomagus.

We arrived in Vindocladia with its white-walled defences and more squared-off Roman-style buildings than I had ever seen in my country before. Some even had red-tiled rooftops like those in Italia. I longed to turn in the other direction, southwest, over the fields and hills towards the sea and our cliffs and our cove. I wanted to go quickly to my own village and find my mother and father, but I could not. Fabia was nursing the younger baby as well as Lucilius, and we had to remain with the Christians. Also I had promised Brica that I would find her family and bring them word from her.

So I stayed for a month there, in a lodging-house, as the Christians dispersed and found places to live. Fabia stayed with the father of the baby she was feeding. She would soon become his wife. She took Lucilius with her, as he was still drinking her milk along with a little solid food. Once they were settled in Vindocladia and I was sure Lucilius was healthy, I was able to leave, and journey, at last, to the place where I was born.

A wagon back to the port where we had landed, and then a riverboat bound for Durnovaria. They told me that to reach the moon cove, I needed to leave the riverboat when it had completed about half its journey, at a certain bridging-point. When we reached that place, I remembered I had been there with my father. I left the river and set off southwards on foot, alone, as no other traveler was going that way.

The sun was high in the sky when I began, though it was often behind the clouds. I walked up the hills and then down, down towards the moon cove. Then I turned east and at last reached our village on the slopes of the hill. It was strange, after so long, to see the familiar shore, the waves coming in over the multitudinous coloured pebbles. Strange to see the high clifftops, the trees in the valley.

The village had grown. In place of the great gathering roundhouse there was a rectangular hall of wood with strong walls, and covered with tiles of stone overlapping in the pattern like a net. And near it, where my father's roundhouse should be, stood another square, tiled house. Everything was similar to the way I remembered it, yet not the same. It seemed as if I were in a dream. In that dream I walked to the house that stood where my father's house should be.

I found there a man who was my brother, a man now, yet with the same face as the boy who learned to write with me, when Cosmas was our teacher. He had married, but his wife died in childbirth along with their infant son. Our little sister and a younger brother born after I left, now both grown, lived nearby. My father had died some years before, but my mother was still alive. My brother led me to her. I found her lying on a couch with her eyes closed, so frail, so thin and old. Then she opened her eyes, and saw me. Suddenly her whole face was filled with enormous joy. The memory I had carried of her grief all those years was wiped away.

After the first embrace and exclamations, we looked at each other, unable to bridge the span of time, not sure how to begin. Slowly we started to make a fabric together of all the lost years.

She told me of how my father died before he could fulfil his aspiration to be a leader on the council in Durnovaria. She said that after my boat was cast off the fish still did not come. The hunger grew worse and they had to kill some of the precious new lambs. The people disagreed about whether the boat sacrifice had been the will of the gods, and the discord grew. At last the Romans commanded Broccomagus and all his allies to leave the place. He never returned.

Meanwhile everything began to change, as many Roman customs spread over the land. The old houses were replaced with new Roman-style buildings. They look strong, said my mother, but will they survive? Were their foundations laid with the proper rituals? Were the corners tied to the earth with the body of a foal or a dog? The new ways are coming too fast, she said.

I told her of my time with Cosmas, my life in Rome, the banishment to Pontia. Then from my traveling chest I brought out the cloth she wove long before. Lucilius was too big for it by then, and I kept it wrapped around this book. I gave the cloth to her and she fingered it gently, touching the threads with their colours of the sea. Then she looked up at me, her eyes full of tears.

She said, I chose the plants, and dyed the wool. I began this weaving so happily, thinking to make a cloak to keep you warm. I imagined seeing you wear it for many winters. And then came the day when I had to snatch it from the loom, so small and so unfinished. I stitched the edge quickly, so I could give it to Cosmas. I hoped he would find your boat out on the sea. I hoped he would take you on the ship, and give you this cloth. So many fragile hopes. And none of them the thing I wanted most and could never hope for: to have you back here with me.

All those years she carried the same sorrow for a vanished child that I carry now.

I told her how I had kept her grandmother's mirror safe in the boat without oars. How I held it tight as I climbed up to the ship, to Cosmas. How he did give me the cloth she wove, and it protected the mirror for many years. And how at last I had to let go of the mirror to pay for our lives. The loss of the mirror grieved her. But she was comforted to know that, after the mirror was gone, I used her cloth to keep Lucilius warm.

I stayed with her, visiting Lucilius in Vindocladia when I could. I did not want him to forget me. Now he could sit up, and crawl, and was trying to babble words. Fabia weaned him early so I could bring him home to my mother.

In her remaining months my mother watched him tenderly as he crawled about. She told me stories of my childhood and that of my brothers and sister. She told tales of her own life. And she passed on to me the old knowledge from her mother and grandmother, the wisdom of plants that heal. She was not well enough to go into the woods and fields, so I tried to find the plants and bring them back to her. I lifted them carefully from the ground in the proper way, as she instructed me. She taught me to name and recognize them and learn their strengths and properties. How many pieces of the herb to use, how to divide them into three times three or nine times nine. She made me promise to pick some particular herbs when midsummer came and they would be at their most powerful. She said she would no longer be with us then.

Lucilius learned to pull himself up by holding on to a stool. She loved to see him stand on his chubby legs.

She said, He is strong. He will survive.

He was taking his first steps when she died, just before spring.

As the months passed, and I still walked unharmed on the forbidden ground, my fear of the druid's curse subsided. He had gone away. His power must have gone with him. The gods of the land no longer did his bidding. Or some other power was stronger than his, and protected me. Was it the goddess Isis? Was it the talisman of the bread and fish that I brought with me? Was it the prayers of the Christians, who had petitioned their god continually during the journey?

One day, not long after I came back to this place, I went down to the sea, and I remembered the stone I had hidden so long ago. I studied the cliff trying to find the place. Then I recognized the rock shaped like a horse's head. I began to climb the cliff above it, with far less ease than when I was a girl. Gradually I pulled myself higher until I saw, right before me, the same crevice, though plants had overgrown the opening. I put my hand

in and stretched out my fingers, feeling in the dark. I touched
something hard. I closed my hand around it, drew my fist out,
and looked at what I held. I gently brushed off the sandy earth.
There was the stone, with my name scratched on it still. Still
safe after all the years. Perhaps that is why no harm had come
to me.

Gradually I made myself at home again, here where I began.
Here where the language is my language, and many other
women have green eyes and tattooed wrists. But I was not the
same as before. I was older, yes. But more than that, Rome and
Pontia had entered into me. They are still part of me now. Everything that happened in those distant places changed me.

I mourned Tilla for a long time. Her death came back to me over
and over. The sickening lurch as she stepped out of the boat.
The soldiers around her fallen body. Her screams.

I was beginning to forget her face. I tried to find her through the
scraps of my memory, and the things of hers I kept through all
my travels: scrolls, a ring, a cloak, and the net of gold thread into
which she used to bundle her hair. But she eluded me.

I missed Lucius too, and the other Christians I knew in Tarracina. Even those who came with me to Britannia are scattered. They stayed in Vindocladia or spread out to Durnovaria
and through the countryside. They were welcomed by some of
the people who were curious about their teaching, as the merchant Corin had said. Others, however, were angry because Felix
wanted to destroy all the old statues and sacred groves. Felix left
altogether with some of his companions and went to Gallia.

A few of the Christians remained in the region. They have
learned the need for patience. And so the old worship places are
still intact. I have often visited the shrine of the mothers and
given thanks there for my son Lucilius. I have also kept the talisman of the bread and fish. I carry it with me always.

I helped my brother with the business of the farm, and made
some of the herbal remedies my mother had taught me. Then
gradually it became known that I could write, and I began to

work as a scribe and translator. But I will never write binding magic. I will not help anyone bring the power of the gods against his or her enemies. Other scribes can have metal tablets at the ready, and write the words of death. I remember too well the horror of bearing a curse on my own head.

Lucilius changed from a baby to a boy, and then into a fine young man. He and I have come to know the sister who was so small when I left, and the little brother I never met. My first brother, who never took another wife or had more children, has treated Lucilius like his own lost son. He wants Lucilius to learn how to manage the land. He also wants him to travel often into Durnovaria and understand the life of the city. Our father was a leader among the people, and my brother is well respected. My brother hopes that one day Lucilius will become important in the city, a decurion perhaps, as my father longed to be. But Lucilius does not like the work of the farm, nor does he want to fulfil my brother's ambitions.

All this time I have kept this old notebook in the chest with the mementoes of Tilla. Only very rarely, in recent years, have I taken it out and leafed through the pages. But now, with Lucilius gone, I prefer to remember the past than to think of the present. The notebook is my companion once more.

All lost things can be restored; only virginity, once lost, can never be restored.

—Saint Nereus to Saint Domitilla

Saint Domitilla, co-patron of Ponza, first-century virgin martyr, shared her feast day of 12th May with Saints Nereus and Achilleus, until she was dropped from the General Roman Calendar in 1969. She is still celebrated on that day in the Eastern Orthodox church, as well as on her island.

According to the early medieval legend, the saints Nereus and Achilleus were Christian stewards of her household, and en-

couraged her choice of virginity. The leaflet from the church on
Ponza omits them, retelling only the part of the legend that in-
volves Domitilla. Fair enough. They have already been clinging
to her hem for too many centuries.

The stories linking their names with hers probably arose because two early Christian martyrs called Nereus and Achilleus
were buried in the place known as the "cemetery of Domitilla."
The cemetery was called this after the woman who owned the
land. A basilica was built in the fourth century over the martyrs'
tombs, and a plaque installed by Pope Damasus was inscribed
with their story. But gradually over the centuries the old cemeter-
ies, or catacombs, were abandoned, and fell into disrepair. As the
original story of Nereus and Achilleus was forgotten, a fabulous
tale developed, connecting them with the tradition of Domitilla
of Ponza, who merged with the Domitilla who gave the land and
her name to the cemetery. The story grew through the centuries,
in many retellings, and with ever more accretions and flourishes,
and is found in many medieval hagiography collections.

Domitilla has two eunuch stewards who are also her guardians, Nereus and Achilleus. She is an orphan who was brought up
as a Christian by her mother, and the stewards are Christian too.
One day they find her in front of the mirror adorning herself in
robes and jewels, preparing for her wedding; and they are horri-
fied. They remind her of the difficulties of marriage; the servi-
tude of wives to their husbands, the way men may be charming at
first, but often change once they bring a woman home, becoming
disrespectful and breaking their marriage vows, and even taking
the household maid to bed. A wife also has to endure the dangers
of childbirth and anxieties of motherhood. But as a virgin, Domitilla will have the beautiful young Christ with her every hour;
he is the only spouse worth considering. Virginity ranks second
only to martyrdom, and will bring her closer to heaven, where
even the air has the scent of virtue, and when your nostrils catch
it, you can feel no sadness. They speak so powerfully of the spiritual and practical advantages of virginity that Domitilla cancels
the wedding.

This enrages her spurned suitor Aurelianus, who has the emperor Domitian send all three into exile on Ponza, along with Domitilla's handmaids Euphrosine and Theodora. When Domitian dies there is a short reprieve during the reign of Nerva; but, under Trajan, Aurelianus's hatred continues to pursue them, and at last they are all imprisoned for their faith at Tarracina (called Terracina today). Nereus and Achilleus are tortured and decapitated.

Domitilla's maids are now also Christian, persuaded by her that the heavenly spouse and the perfumes of celestial meadows are superior to marriage. Aurelianus dies suddenly from too much dancing, and the women are suspected of causing this somehow. All three are locked in a house and the house is set on fire. Their bodies are found the next day, untouched by the flames, lying face down as they fell while the women prayed. They are buried deep in the earth, in Terracina. Their memory is honoured because of their fierce willingness to die rather than yield their virginity to any man.

Losing my virginity to Franco and becoming pregnant was, to the world and to my mother, my great mistake. I thought so too, before the baby was born. There were twisted layers of shame; the shame of losing the world's approval and, even worse, my mother's. There was the sorrow of ruining all she had worked for, all her hopes for me.

She took it for granted from the beginning that I would give the baby up. She only visited me at the maternity home once; it was after the baby was born, but my mother refused to see her. We met in the sitting room; the baby was sleeping upstairs. In the middle of outlining briskly how I would soon be home and studying again, she paused; and I tried feebly to say something about keeping the baby.

"Oh, don't be so foolish," she said, "How on earth would you be able to do that?"

Although I realised it too late, my real mistake was that I let my daughter go. I did not know that the disgrace of unmarried motherhood would later seem trivial compared with this life-long guilt. I abandoned my child. I should have fought to keep her.

For some girls, adoption may have been the right thing. But I should have done what all my instincts urged me to do. My body and mind and heart were wrapped up in her; but I did not know how to make that focus fierce enough. I was bewildered, and I was young. I was a passionate new mother; and at the same time I wanted to be a good girl again. And so I did what I was told, I let them take my child away.

Yet my mother herself had brought up a baby on her own; but with the crucial, all-important difference that she had been married when she conceived me. She always wore the wedding ring. She could, and I suspect did, imply to the inquisitive that her husband had died in the war, rather than explain his abandonment.

Some years later, I tried to talk to her about the past. I told her I had really loved Franco and it was not my fault he treated me as he did.

She said, "It was a vulgar affair with a man who seduced you and used you—I thought you knew better than that." In a few words tarnishing for ever, even more than he already had done himself, our time together.

Now, of course, I am older than she was then. After I have seen so many girls and women throw themselves away on untrustworthy males, goodness knows I can understand her point of view. Yet I also have a tenderness for my lost self, that foolish girl who really was in love, and who trusted the feeling, trusted the moment, trusted him.

For the rest of my mother's life our relationship was civil, but not intimate. And so I was taken aback when right at the end, not long before she died, she said, "I wish I had been a grandmother." And after a pause, in which I was silent, she went on, "Well, of course, I was a grandmother once. I suppose biologically speaking I still am. Sometimes I wonder about that child," she said, and she looked at me. I could not answer. It seemed impossible to touch the forbidden subject after so much time. So she spoke of something else. The moment was lost; I wish I knew what she might have said, had I given her the chance.

She died six years ago—nearly seven, now; it was the year before I first learned of Marina's manuscript. I have been thinking more and more about my daughter. I have been trying to rid myself of a longstanding dread of her scorn for me, a mother who was no mother to her. Recently I have been imagining that perhaps, on my next trip back to England, I would try to find out at least whether she has made any inquiries. She was eighteen in 1985, and since then has been legally allowed to search for her birth parents. Her search, if she began it, will not have been successful. I never reported her father's identity, he was registered as "Unknown;" and she would have been searching for me under my real name, the name I had when she was born. I was not Aubrey then, but Avril Jones, about to be twenty-three. I was named for my birth month, April; and she was born in April too, on the seventeenth, a few days before my own birthday. She shadowed every April afterwards.

If only it were true that all lost things can be restored. I can never recover the years I have not known my own child. I can never watch her grow from a baby to a girl to a young woman. All that is lost to me.

While thinking more about her in the last few years, and especially in the last year, since it became legal for me also to initiate a search, I was naturally assuming that there was plenty of time. I had ages ahead, I thought, in which to attempt to tie up the loose threads of my life. But now I have had to accept this new reality of my illness, and learn what the doctors can do, and what they cannot. I thought I was strong enough to confront the past and its consequences; but all my strength has gone into facing the present instead.

My trips to the hospital for various therapies have alternated with the writing of this book, and the work has sustained me. It has become part of my life, intimately linked with it like the *tegula* and *imbrex* tiles of an ancient Roman—and modern Italian—roof. But now the doctors have done all they are able, and I think there is very little time remaining.

In these days of the worldwide web, I know, many questions can be answered at a distance. At school all the students and several teachers use the Internet continually, and indeed I sometimes consult it myself for research. But I am not at home there; it is too new and strange a domain for me. Probably web places exist where one can search for lost children, but it is too late for me to learn to navigate them now.

Now I can only reach out to her through the pages of this book.

⁓

The harvest is over, the days are cooler. Lucilius has not come back. But something else has happened, something extraordinary. Everything I thought was true is not true at all. Everything has changed.

A traveler from Italia is visiting the Christians here, and he has brought something I never imagined I would see: a letter from Tilla. She is alive. She wrote it a few months ago.

I will transcribe her words:

Flavia Domitilla to Marina of Britannia and Lucilius Flavius Clemens:

Marina, after all these years, dear sister, I greet you and hope that you are in good health. I write this with my own hand holding the pen, so you might see I have not forgotten the lessons you gave me.

Did you look back, when you left Pontia in the boat with my baby Lucilius? Did you see me fall, surrounded by soldiers with drawn swords? They hit me with the flat of their swordblades, they tied my wrists, they forced me to climb back up to the villa, still bleeding from the birth, my breasts dripping with new milk. They called me whore and filth, they threatened to violate me and kill me. But in the end they did neither. I think the young soldier—the one who warned us—somehow dissuaded them. They told me to leave the villa and hide myself away.

Glauca and Philemon had been beaten cruelly for refusing to say where we were when the baby was born. Yet now they helped me find a place to hide, and they cared for me. Time passed. My fever cooled, my body healed. But I had lost everything all over again, and more than I had ever lost before.

I thought the soldiers would kill me quickly. I did not imagine my suffering would last for years. At first, I wanted to die, yet lacked the courage to kill myself. Every day, for months, I expected the soldiers to come and carry out the emperor's command. I was only grateful that my baby was not there. I would not have to see them dash his head against the wall or spit him on their swords.

Yet I wanted him so much. My breasts were full of his milk for many days. My arms never stopped aching for him.

And I missed you, Marina, my sister, my friend.

What sustained me was something very strange. It was the power that told me to step out of the boat: a voice that did not speak, a presence I could not see. But it was real, and it stayed with me. It comforted me. I know now it was the spirit of Iesous.

When Domitianus died and Nerva became emperor, many exiles were pardoned. But not those, like me, related to Domitianus. He has been declared "of cursed memory." However, I was no longer in danger of death, and there were new soldiers at the garrison. I moved to these rooms near the harbour.

There is a Christian ecclesia now on Pontia. It began when Lucius, Dorothea, and Zoë were here, living in the port while you and I were up on the headland. Many people complained against them, but a very small group adopted their way in secret. It has slowly grown with visits from other sisters and brothers. They have helped me to live, and to find some reason for living.

For a long time, I was possessed by the desire to see you and the baby again. I thought it was only to be sure that you were both safe, but I was deceiving myself. Really I wanted to reclaim Lucilius as my own. But by the time I learned that you lived in Tarracina, you had already left for Britannia.

Marina, I am dying. I want you to know you were right to take Lucilius and leave me behind on Pontia. I thank you with all my heart for taking him safely away.

And I want you to know you did well to go to a distant place, to take him back to your country. Once I understood he was so far off, I was able to relinquish him at last. I accepted that he was your son, and I was glad of it. I knew that you would keep him safe.

Lucilius, if you survived your infancy and childhood, you will be almost a young man now. Perhaps Marina has told you of how I had to let you go, and why. I want you to know that I did it only to save your life.

Although you were just a few days old then, I had loved you before you were born. I loved you when you were growing inside me and I felt you move. After your birth, I loved you even more. Sitting in that boat with the soldiers coming closer, I knew I could not bear to see them kill you. I found the strength—or rather, it was sent to me—to give myself up, and step out of the boat.

All the years since then, Lucilius, I have held you in my thoughts. I have prayed for your health. And I have prayed that no spirits of evil temper might enter you, and drive out your spirit of goodness. For as the Shepherd told Hermas, and as Hermas wrote in his book, a person filled with evil spirits has lost his way, and wanders here and there, as if blind.

I go to the next world trusting that you are a young man who sees clearly. I also trust you will do all in your power not to cause Marina, your mother, any sorrow.

Be well: live in God. May you be written in the book of life.

Thus writes Tilla. And so she has been alive all this time, on Pontia. The man who brought the letter said she is known to possess gifts of knowledge and of healing from Iesous.

All these years she has been alive on Pontia, while I traveled further and further away with her child.

When he was small he used to ask me about his real mother, and his father. I said only that his mother was a brave girl who loved him, and his father was of a fine family. The right time never seemed to come to tell him the whole story. Then he stopped asking.

Now I do not know where he is. I can send no messenger to tell him of this letter. I can only wait until he comes back. Then he will see the letter with his own eyes. He will trace with his fingers the ink of the words she wrote for him.

After that I will put this very notebook into his hands. He will, or so I hope, read all I have written, the pages of his mother's story, and the story of his own beginning. Then at last he will reach this page, this very page I am writing on, these very words. So now, Lucilius, I speak to you, even if only with my pen, because I cannot yet see you face to face.

Although I call you my son, you have always known I am not the woman who gave birth to you. I told you her name was Tilla, and she loved you, and she died bravely. But I could never tell how I left her there under the flash of swords.

I love you as much as any true mother could. I loved you from the moment I saw you enter the world. I began trying to keep you safe as soon as you were born. I spoke the old words of protection over you as my own mother did over me. Tilla smiled at the strange sounds she did not understand.

Now you yourself speak that same language. I brought you to this place far from your ancestors because I believed she was dead. It seemed the best way to keep you safe. I wish I could have seen her again. I wish she could have seen you, and you could have known her. But Lucilius, read her words: see how she has loved you all this time. We have both loved you, she from a distance, and I close at hand. You are her son, and you are mine. You are of Italia and of Britannia. In you, Roman and British ways are joined together.

You escaped death on Pontia and many times afterwards. Surely your life is not destined to end now in some mead-soaked brawl? Every day is shorter than the last, Lucilius, and the coldest nights of winter are near.

Come back.

. . . we afterwards took up his bones, as being more precious than the most exquisite jewels, and more purified than gold, and deposited them in a fitting place. . . .

—*The Martyrdom of Polycarp*

While working on Marina's manuscript, I studied the legends of Domitilla to see how they grew from the kernel of reality. One day I found myself in a library in Rome, the Biblioteca Vallicelliana, next to the church of Santa Maria in Vallicella. This church, also known as Chiesa Nuova since Saint Philip Neri rebuilt it in the sixteenth century, is the motherhouse of the Oratorians, the congregation Saint Philip founded in 1556. The nucleus of the library is the collection of books owned by Neri himself; later legacies expanded the holdings. Here are the works of church historians through centuries, as well as studies in patristics, martryology, hagiography, and more.

The librarian brought the volume I had requested, a miscellany of writings by the Oratorian priest and scholar Antonio Gallonio. It was an early printed book, almost four hundred years old, imposingly fat, with heavy leather covers. The librarian placed it on the bookrest, and I turned its stiff pages reverently, admiring the antique typeface sprinkled with the long "s." The Italian text was laid out in columns, an echo of the days of the scroll; there were two columns on each page.

Gathered in this volume were several works on saints by Gallonio, including two versions of the story of Nereus, Achilleus and Domitilla. Gallonio first wrote about Domitilla in his 1591 *Holy Virgins of Rome*. This book was in Italian rather than Latin so more people could read these edifying tales of women who consecrated themselves to virginity. The chapter entitled "Saints Flavia Domitilla, Euphrosine, and Theodora, Roman virgin martyrs" is illustrated with an engraving of a house surrounded by roaring flames, and the women praying inside. Gallonio specialized in hagiography; he wrote of modern saints as well as ancient ones, writing biographies of his contemporaries Philip Neri and

Roman virgin Elena de' Massimi, who died at only thirteen. He bridged time, showing that the same patterns of sanctity appear across the centuries, inspired by the same timeless God.

He also wrote a book about the instruments of torture used in martyrdoms. This required much historical and medical research into the horrifying details. Repulsive though the topic of that work seems today, the method reflects a growing trend in his time to approach history with a new rigour, carefully sifting evidence, and documenting references and sources, secular as well as ecclesiastical.

Gallonio's second version of the Domitilla legend was written in 1597 as a stand-alone work. He was asked to produce this for a particular reason by Cesare Baronio, now the superior of the congregation.

Baronio was himself an ecclesiastical historian. The Protestant reformers claimed that Catholic traditions were all myth and superstition; so Baronio, at Neri's request, embarked on the colossal task of gathering historical evidence for early Christian lives, congregations, and saints. Between 1588 and 1607 he published twelve volumes of his church history. In this work he mentioned Flavius Clemens, and the two Flavia Domitillas, his wife and niece, both Christians, both exiled. It seems to have been Baronio who first insisted, with reference to the sources, that there were two separate Christian Flavia Domitillas: the older married one, wife of Flavius Clemens, sent to Pandateria; and the younger, virgin Domitilla, niece of Clemens, sent to Ponza.

Baronio was made a cardinal in 1596. Every cardinal was, and still is, assigned a church in Rome as his titular church. He asked for an ancient one in a damp place near the Baths of Caracalla, in desperate need of restoration. According to the records, it had been dedicated to Nereus and Achilleus since at least 595; rather unusually, since it was nowhere near their burial place in the cemetery of Domitilla. But it seems knowledge of their tombs and basilica had been lost by Baronio's day; perhaps the place was inaccessible after the invasions by the Goths or the Lombards, or it was damaged in an earthquake, or just became overgrown and buried like the other catacombs in the city. At that time, some catacombs had just been rediscovered, and there was great interest in them and in their early Christian relics and paintings. Philip Neri himself used to pray in one of them. In 1593 the young Antonio Bosio, the "Columbus of the Catacombs," whom Baronio knew, had actually explored the catacomb of Domitilla; but he thought it was part of a different cemetery.

Baronio knew the story connecting Nereus and Achilleus with Domitilla, and mentions them in his church history as Domitilla's eunuch advisors, killed in Terracina. He knew the twenty-eighth homily of Pope Gregory the Great, who in the sixth century spoke of Nereus and Achilleus at the very site of their tombs. But he seems not to have known that those tombs were in the cemetery of Domitilla. He thought this damp ruined church named for them was where they were buried, and where Gregory preached.

Baronio rescued the church, restored it in what he considered an Early Christian style, and had it decorated with frescoes telling the story of Nereus, Achilleus and Domitilla, all linked together as in the now highly developed legend. Domitilla was not mentioned in the church's dedication, but Baronio placed her at the heart of the story. Around this time, she was united with Nereus and Achilleus in the calendar as well, as her feast day was moved from its earlier date of May 7th to theirs, May 12th.

Baronio received Papal permission to gather the relics of these three saints and take them to his restored church. Several Roman churches had such relics, most importantly San Adriano. This was an ancient building in the Forum, once the Roman senate house, later a Christian church. The bodies of Nereus and Achilleus had been deposited there in the early 1200s, as an inscription testified. Perhaps they were transferred directly from their original tombs; or they may have been exhumed earlier, and spent the interim centuries elsewhere. The church claimed to have the body and head of Domitilla as well as those of Nereus and Achilleus, although the legend says she died separately. But as the three were inextricably joined in legend, so their remains somehow came together.

According to a contemporary account, Baronio went to San Adriano with witnesses. Four priests welcomed him, lamps were lit, and the relics were taken from their place of safekeeping. The three heads of the martyrs reposed in separate wooden reliquaries decorated with gold. One of the priests solemnly swore, hand on heart, that the bodies and heads had been found, with very old inscriptions, by Cardinal Cusano of San Adriano, during the church's recent restoration; and that Cusano had arranged for the heads to be enclosed in the reliquaries. In the Latin text the word for these reliquaries is *capsa*, or sometimes *theca*, the same word Marina uses for her writing box.

Baronio piously received the relics and took them away. This process was repeated elsewhere, as he collected other remains of Nereus, Achilleus and Domitilla scattered around Rome. They were then placed under the altar of the restored church of Nereus and Achilleus on their feast day in 1597 with a procession and much ceremony. It was to celebrate this that Baronio asked Gallonio for a new Italian edition of the story of the saints.

Gallonio puts Nereus and Achilleus in the title with Domitilla this time: *Story of the Life and Martyrdom of the Glorious Saints Flavia Domitilla, Virgin, Nereus and Achilleus, and Others*. He changes the order of telling, making it clearer, he says, and he includes the recent translation of the saints' relics to their restored church. He dedicates the work in flowery language, on a beautifully illustrated dedication page, to Cardinal Baronio.

In the way of historians and hagiographers, he pieced together details from different sources. He gave the saints speeches and gestures, as if to reanimate the relics, as if to reclothe them with flesh and make them living men and women for the faithful to admire. I have taken no such liberties here, but there is something I should admit. At the beginning of this notebook, I mentioned lacunae in Marina's manuscript, missing parts and illegible words. If this were a scholarly work, I would have indicated these at the appropriate moments in Marina's text, and left gaps in my translation. But it is far from being scholarly, and instead I have made my own best guess, in those places, at what was on the page before time and insects and damp destroyed the text and sometimes the parchment itself. This is just one more irregularity, in a very irregular book, for the scholar to forgive.

But this time I am not writing for the approval of scholars. I realise now that I care only about a more personal kind of mercy: the forgiveness of one particular reader. I dedicate this book to her.

Lucilius came back at last.

Before he came back I had received word through the network of Christians that Tilla had died peacefully in her sleep.

I was surprised at the change in him. He had grown a little taller, his beard was darker, and his body was more lean and strong.

I told him that his mother had been alive, and had written a letter for him. But now she was dead.

I gave him her letter. There it was, in his hands. They are the hands of a man now, and they held the thin wooden tablets tenderly, as he read the ink-written words of a mother he has never known. Here at last he has some reward for having studied the hated Roman arts of the pen.

Tell me about her, he said.

I gave him this notebook. He took it away and read it, right up to those last words I wrote.

Then he wanted me to tell him more, anything else I could remember. We spoke about Tilla for a long time.

He kept asking, Why did you bring me to this place? Why did you bring me so far away from her? It is your fault I never knew my real mother.

He has been filled with restlessness ever since, and now he has disappeared again. He said no word about where he was going or what he intends to do.

He has taken Tilla's letter.

I am in despair. I am afraid her sacrifice was in vain. I am afraid she stepped out of the boat and gave herself up to the soldiers for nothing. I fear Lucilius will die now, on the very edge of manhood. He is reckless and his companions are worse. They ride far to taunt the Romans in their garrisons, they damage new buildings and the barracks of the legions. Surely the Romans will kill him, or conscript him and send him to the wars.

I am afraid I will never see him again.

The more you mow us down, the more our numbers increase. The blood of Christians is seed.

—Tertullian, *Apoligeticus*

Nearly three hundred years after Baronio installed the relics in his titular church, the archaeologist Guiseppe B. De Rossi discovered, while excavating the Catacomb of Domitilla in 1874, the original tombs and fourth-century basilica of Nereus and Achilleus. He also found part of the long-lost ancient inscription; it was broken, but medieval travelers had seen it *in situ* and written it down, so the text could be reconstructed. This was the inscription set up by Pope Damasus, whose papacy ran from 366 to 384, and it gives a completely different account of Nereus and Achilleus. There is no mention of Domitilla in this earlier tradition. Nereus and Achilleus were Roman soldiers, killed because they gave up their weapons to become Christian. The early Christians considered soldiering incompatible with their faith, and Diocletian began persecuting Christians who refused to bear arms in the late 200s. If this was the real story of Nereus and Achilleus, they could not have known Domitilla; they lived about two centuries too late.

Now the whole early medieval romance of Nereus and Achilleus as Domitilla's eunuch guardians fell apart. The saint of Ponza appeared more and more legendary. Because Baronio had been wrong in accepting her connection with Nereus and Achilleus, many scholars thought everything else he said about Domitilla of Ponza was wrong too, including the idea that she was the younger of two exiled Flavia Domitillas sent to different islands.

She was seen more and more as a fictional product of the church's cult of virginity. Such was the fascination with beautiful young virgin martyrs who gave their souls to Christ, and their bodies to gruesome deaths, that some early hagiographers bestowed virginity on women who had been married and even had children. But Flavia Domitilla, wife of Flavius Clemens and mother of seven children, was too well known to history to be transformed into a virgin; and so, it has been thought, the younger, virgin Domitilla was conjured up alongside her. And, for Baronio and Gallonio, her medieval story seemed of authentic antiquity, and fitted their Counter-Reformation zeal and their Oratorian interest in an earlier, purer Christianity.

However, a few scholars felt that this solution left unanswered questions. What about the older testimony of Jerome and Eusebius, and the ancient memory on Ponza of a Christian Domitilla, long venerated by the people of the island? Nereus and Achilleus had dropped out of her story, where they never belonged in the first place; this did not prove that the original Domitilla tradition was a hagiographical fantasy. These few have refused to discard the saint of Ponza, the younger Domitilla. And now Marina has vindicated them.

Yes, the legends turned Tilla too into a virgin. Her true story was altered, and embellished; but a faint memory of the living, breathing, woman did survive. And why does Terracina feature so prominently in the story, why does Domitilla die there? Perhaps the legend preserves, beneath its ornate accretions, an echo of the promise made by the Terracina Christians that they would always remember Tilla.

And so she joined the company of martyrs, who from the earliest days, like Polycarp of Smyrna, Alban of Britain, Perpetua in Carthage, and Blandina in Lyon, chose to suffer brutal killing rather than sacrifice to other gods. Surely they could have given a pinch of incense or a few drops of the libation, as a mere formality, and in their hearts remained true? They could not. Their

lunatic courage astounds us now. Their zeal to die seems un-
healthy, and so does the grisly relish with which their stories have
been told over and over. But sometimes I wish I could believe that
fiercely in something.

Five nights have passed since I last wrote.

My despair is changed to great joy, for Lucilius has returned.

I was sure he had gone off to seek his old companions. But he
went, alone, to the sea to find a ship. He planned to work for
his passage and somehow reach Italia, and the island of Pontia.
He wanted to see where Tilla had lived and died. He wanted to
return to where he was born, where his life began.

He reached the harbour where we landed when we came back
to Britannia, when he was still a baby. He looked for a ship, and
could not find one that would take him. In this season few ships
sail. The days went by. He had to work so he could eat. As he
unloaded cargoes and knotted ropes, Tilla's letter was always in
his mind. He had memorized the words she wrote for him, and
he spoke them to himself. Sometimes he took the letter from
where he kept it safe, and read it again.

And then he decided to come back home.

He assured me that he had not come back because he was afraid
to go on the voyage. He stood there telling me this, edgy and
proud, determined I should not think him cowardly. Indeed, he
has none of my fear of the sea. I have tried to hide it from him.
He handles a boat in our coastal waters with great skill.

He said, I still would like to travel to Pontia when the time is
right. But not yet.

And he told me he had earned some of his meals in a metal
workshop. He said, The smith showed me how to heat and
shape the metal. He made nails and brooches and horse trappings and things for ships. He knew all the old engraving patterns, and the stories in them. I do not want to work with my

uncle waiting for crops to grow and counting the heads of my cattle. I want to be a maker of things. I want to make things that endure.

Here, he said, and he handed me a lopsided bronze bowl. He showed me where he had scratched *Lucilius fecit* on the base.

Some day, he said, I will make you a mirror as fine as the one you gave for our passage.

I have seen the sun break through
to illuminate a small field, and gone my way
and forgotten it. But that was the pearl
of great price, the one field that had
the treasure in it.

—R.S. Thomas, *The Bright Field*

I began this notebook last October; it is April now. My daughter's thirty-first birthday approaches, and then my fifty-fifth, and after that will come, yet again, the anniversary of the day I let her go.

What she might think of me does not matter any more; I must send these words on the journey I can no longer undertake.

We don't fully realise, when we drop things addressed to England in the mailbox, or hand them over the post office desk, that they will actually have to cross the Atlantic, whether by plane or ship, the real grey endless Atlantic with its waves and storms and treacherous deeps.

I will post this notebook to Mr Hughes, the curator, at the museum in Dorset where he works now. I will send it just as I have written it, in my own hand, and in my half-American, half-British English, which I trust no one will tamper with, nor try to wrench into conformity with one or the other idiom, for this is my language now: it speaks of my life.

I never went back to the Mendips for fear everything would be different from the way I remember. Especially I remember one small field, closely enfolded by hills. The depth of the greenness is startling. The field has been left fallow; thistles and cornflowers and Queen Anne's lace are growing there, amidst the green grass. The late sun fills the field with light for just a moment before dropping behind the hill.

Now, if I could, I would go back, unafraid, to reclaim the past; not with the impossible idea of living in it, but to let it rest. I would want to accept the whole life of that field, just as it is and however much it has changed, past and present and future.

The curator will know what to do about Marina's story, and about my own. He knows about preservation; he knows about tracing connections. Through him, I believe, Marina's words will reach the scholars, and mine will reach my daughter, somehow, wherever she is.

Wherever you are, my little girl, I wonder if you know about the clothes I dressed you in, knitted by a kind old lady for the home. I chose a shell pink sweater and leggings set. The stitches spread to openwork over your chubby thighs. I washed the last traces of my milk from your mouth, arranged your dark wisps of hair, and wrapped you in your blanket. In the blanket's folds I tucked a letter. It said that I loved you, and would have kept you if I could. I signed it "your mother."

Then Mrs White came and took you from my arms before I was ready; I tried to follow her downstairs, I screamed for her to wait, and she made one of the staff members drag me back inside the room where, just a minute before, I had you with me still. After a while I heard the front door slam and I went to the window, I looked down and saw a man and a woman walking away from the house, and the woman was carrying a bundle. I fell to the floor under the windowsill, but it was too late: I had seen. I had seen the woman, and the bundle that was you, one of your small hands sticking out from the blanket, a little of your dark hair just visible, her arms tight around you: I would keep on seeing that, over and over again.

Did they keep the clothes? Did they show you my letter, when you were old enough?

I called you Cara. Did they keep your name?

If you have read this, Cara, *carissima*, you still may not be able to forgive, but I hope you will at least understand. When I bought this beautiful book in Florence, with its leather spine and its endpapers patterned like the mesh of a net or the foamy lace on a wave, I had no idea what I might write in it. Years later, when I had finished work on Marina's manuscript and wanted to make a kind of annotation of her story, I chose this book, because it seemed to have been waiting for a special destiny, and because it is large enough to allow me the space I knew I would need. I began gathering the scattered fragments and putting them together, as the caddis fly nymph collects pebbles and glues them onto its back as camouflage.

What I could not know was how Marina and Tilla and Lucilius would step out of their past and help me to understand my own. What I could not imagine was how the truth of my life would emerge in the mosaic of these pages.

Although I did not realise it when I began, I see now that I have been writing for you all along: this is your book.

I last wrote as winter came; now it is spring. I am reaching the end of these pages that I began as an exile on Pontia in a distant time.

I am with my own people now, and they call me by the name I was given on the clifftop long ago. Now writing is more a custom in this land, and I write the names of my people in a less Roman way, closer to how we speak them. The name of my aunt, Lavinia, who died before I returned, would now be written: Lovernisca. It comes from our word for that swift animal, the fox. My own name, the name she found for me, the name that means She-Who-Is-Born-of-the-Sea, I write thus: Morigena. But to Romans, travelers, and foreigners, I am Marina; both names are mine.

It seems to me that there are invisible strands through the universe, always moving, like the eels in the fish pools of Pontia: a net of intercurving living ribbons.

These strands knot together people from one side of the world to the other, connecting those dead to those alive and those as yet unborn. What or who guides the design I do not claim to know. Whether Iesous is friend to Apollo and to Belenos, or whether they are all enemies, whether Isis of the many names is the sister of our Three Mothers, I cannot tell. But I know invisible forces touched Tilla, and saved Lucilius and me. I know the strong protection of the seacliffs sheltered my namestone and kept me safe until I could return. I know some benign power quenched the druid's curse.

I look at the green hills rising around me, and the trees with their roots deep in the earth. I go down to where the everlasting sea crashes over the stones, and I remember the three dolphin messengers. I see the deer running through the deep woods, fleet in their own domain. And I know the gods will always be in the land.

Lucilius has been protected, and he has survived to young manhood. And because he fled to the harbour when the letter from Tilla came, and worked with the metalsmith there, I have made a new friend. This metalworker makes good and useful and beautiful things.

He is a trustworthy man. I believe he will bring joy to all my remaining seasons.

Look after this book when I am gone, Lucilius. Keep it well gathered and tied. Take care of the worn leather covers, and respect the good craftsmanship of Secundus in Rome. Sew up the stitching, should it loosen. Bind all the pages together.

Keep this story safe for your children and your children's children, this story of both your mothers: Tilla, who lived and died in distant Italy. And Marina, whose life will end in the place where she was born.

When you hold this book in your hand, you are holding something of Tilla and of me.

I, Marina Morigena of Britannia, finish this book
early in winter.

Eternity is a mysterious absence of times and ages; an endless length of ages always present, and for ever perfect.
—Thomas Traherne, *Centuries of Meditations*

In Rome, I went in search of the physical remains of Saint Domitilla of Ponza. The custodian in the church of Nereus and Achilleus by the Baths of Caracalla still holds to the legend of Domitilla and her eunuch stewards, as illustrated in the frescoes Baronio commissioned. In front of the altar there is a grille over a hole in the floor. Apparently the remains of the martyrs still lie under the slab of stone just visible below.

But not their complete remains. Not their heads. From various researches I learned that the heads of Nereus and Achilleus were moved from this church to the Chiesa Nuova soon after the restoration and translation. Was Domitilla's head taken there as well?

When Baronio restored his titular church, he asked the Pope if it might be given into the care of his congregation, the Oratorians of the Chiesa Nuova, and it is still administered by them today. So this is the link between Nereus, Achilleus and Domitilla and the Chiesa Nuova, and the reason for the Rubens painting of these three saints in the enormous baroque church.

The Chiesa Nuova is the church Saint Philip Neri built and where his body lies. It holds many relics of his, including shoes and shirts. There are chapels commemorating the ecstasy he was glimpsed in while celebrating the Eucharist, and the moment when, as he prayed in the catacomb of Saint Sebastian, his heart suddenly expanded so violently that his ribs broke. There is marble and gilt and opulence everywhere. These surroundings seem at odds with the modesty of Philip himself, who was known for his love of the poor, his humility, and his good humour, as well as his interest in an earlier, simpler Christianity. And indeed, the baroque decorations were added after his death; he had wanted the church to be white and plain.

The Rubens painting is all well and good; but I do not think this satin-robed woman with a head full of blonde curls, her eyes turned piously heavenward, can bear any resemblance to Tilla as she was in real life, fifteen hundred years before Rubens picked up a paintbrush.

When I inquired about a relic of the head of Saint Domitilla, I was sent to a young Padre who led me into the sacristy, his cassock swirling around his legs as he strode briskly across the marbled floors. He told me he did not think the church possessed Saint Domitilla's head. The sacristy was a large room with cupboards of rich dark wood all along the walls, from floor to ceiling. He took from a drawer a chart of the cupboards, or *armadii*, with a list of the contents of each one, and he was surprised to see that, according to this chart, the head of Domitilla was kept in Armadio Sette. This seventh cupboard was in the upper row; to reach it the priest had to climb athletically onto a narrow ledge. Standing up there in his cassock, he opened the door and peered in, like a housemaid looking for linens. I could see reliquaries of gold and silver, encrusted with ornamentation. He read the names: Nereus, Achilleus, Ursula.

Suddenly he said, *Ecco*, Here is Domitilla, and he lifted down a heavy reliquary, about two feet high and almost two and a half feet wide, with an ornate golden lid and a glass front. Behind the glass was a riot of jeweled flowers and gold; there was almost too much confectionery to see the relics. Then I recognized two leg bones, one across the top of the reliquary and the other across the bottom; both were labeled "artemii," so these belonged to Saint Artemius. But there, in the center of the reliquary, was a skull, with a garland of flowers made from jewels around it, and on it a golden tag: *caput flaviae domitillae.*

I stared at the relic, wishing there were a way to know that the most unlikely thing was true, that she really inhabited this ancient orb of bone, that it was really part of the bodily shell of Domitilla of Ponza, Marina's Tilla, even though she died and was buried on the island, even though there is no reason for her head to be separated from her body, or for any part of her to be in Rome at all.

And yet it must be admitted that there is no evidence of her tomb anywhere; the only traces of her on Ponza in Jerome's time were the cells where she had lived. Perhaps Christians did gather up what remains they could from her burial place on Ponza, and bring them back to Rome. Many other relics have made far stranger journeys.

FINIS.

I, Carol Baker, write these words here at the very end of Aubrey's book, the book she calls mine. It has come safely into my hands at last, as she hoped it would.

The curator, Robert Hughes, received in the post her package from America containing this notebook. He tried to contact her, but learned she had died in a hospice soon after sending it.

I here record my deep gratitude to him for searching until he found me, and for giving me this book; and to my birth mother Aubrey, or Avril, for writing these pages, and so answering the questions I have carried all my life. For I never knew about the letter she wrote, or the clothes she dressed me in before giving me up; everything that came from her had been discarded.

Mr Hughes intends to study and collate Aubrey's papers. He also hopes to discover the identity of the archaeologist and whereabouts of the original manuscript. He will make Marina's text known to the world, as Aubrey wanted.

Here in the back of the manuscript of my mother's book, as if this way she could know about it, I will keep the photograph Mr Hughes has given me. Marina's story reminded him of something he saw once among the miscellanea in the museum's basement. After a long search, he found it and photographed it: a fragment of Roman-British metalwork that has been in the museum for over a century, provenance unknown. It is a broken piece of bronze with curvilinear decoration and basketwork design like that on British Iron Age mirrors. From the fragment's shape, it appears to be part of a mirror. And it bears an inscription: *Lucilius fecit*.

C. Baker, May 12, 1999

Author's Note

A book like this one raises the question of how much is history and how much is the author's invention.

All the epigraphs Aubrey/Avril uses are real, and so is all the historical information in her parts of the book. This includes the controversy surrounding the woman, or women, called Flavia Domitilla, which Aubrey has, I hope, described more or less accurately. One scholar's declaration that the putative younger exiled Domitilla "may safely be discarded" compelled in me a passionate desire to salvage her. Of the possible answers to the puzzle, I chose, or rather my story demanded, the currently least preferred solution: that there were two exiled women called Flavia Domitilla, one sent to Pandateria (now Ventotene), and one to Ponza, and that the younger evolved into Ponza's Saint Domitilla. Although this is the answer I like best, it also seems more logical to me, given the early and enduring memory of a Christian Domitilla on Ponza, as testified to by Jerome and Eusebius. The work of some modern scholars, for example the late Marta Sordi, supports this view.

I tried to make sure this telling of what could have happened did not contradict anything we know. I have tried not to change any history, only to fill in some gaps.

The real reasons why Domitian exiled Flavia Domitilla, or both women if there were two, are unknown; as the emperor was no model of rectitude, there is room for my idea that he killed the consul Flavius Clemens, and exiled the consul's wife, to cover up his abuse of the younger Domitilla, rather than because of their interest in Christianity—though that made a good excuse. There is a (disputed) church tradition that he did persecute Christians.

Although my character Tilla is posited as the kernel of truth inside the lore of the saint, I've imagined that her pregnancy and her baby's birth were never widely known, and were forgotten by the Christians as they venerated her life. Eventually she acquired that important attribute of a young female saint of the early church: virginity.

There are two different strands of story about her death, and I have sought to reconcile them. The early medieval legends have Domitilla and her maidservants dying at Terracina. In my story, that's because Marina had friends in the Terracina community who knew her and Tilla on Ponza, and who then took her in when she arrived fresh from witnessing Tilla's courage and apparent death. I've imagined that they honoured the memory of Tilla in Terracina for centuries, and that this gave rise to stories that she actually died there. In reality, it is unknown why hagiography has Domitilla and her maidservants dying in Terracina, though the Bollandist notes on the *Acta Sanctorum* do mention ancient records (presumably now lost, if they existed) of Nereus, Achilleus and Domitilla from the Terracina church. The other, earlier, strand is the one Jerome knew: she lived on Ponza in a "long martyrdom." Neither he nor Eusebius ever mentioned a horrific martyr's death in Terracina. So I have given her many years on Ponza, and a peaceful end there.

Whether and how her remains really reached Rome is unknown. But I have seen the reliquary enclosing the skull labeled *caput domitillae flaviae*.

Marina/Morigena is my creation, and so is her diary, but I have tried to keep the notebook itself and its contents within the bounds of the historically accurate, or at least the possible. The physical survival of the entire first-century manuscript does, I confess, stretch those bounds to the limit. But fragments of papyrus and parchment codices have been dated to the first and second centuries, so it seems just possible that in the right circumstances a whole early codex could survive, as did the twelve papyrus Nag Hammadi codices from a couple of centuries later, and the vellum Codex Sinaiticus from the mid-fourth century.

Scholars say that a person in ancient Rome would not have kept a journal, in our sense of the word, because it demands an introspection and awareness of individuality alien to the ancient mindset. However, Roman authors like Pliny the Younger and Tacitus do refer to notebooks, commentaries, and memoirs written by people they knew. Unfortunately, most of these are lost. While I have striven not to give Marina any specifically modern attitudes—though that is ultimately impossible, as I cannot dismantle my own worldview—I feel that she might have written an account of her days. She grew up far from the literate milieu of ancient Rome, she came fresh to the art of writing, and perhaps she had a different sense of its conventions. On Ponza, she begins writing to calm herself with the familiar movements and to pass the time; surely she might gradually come to find the notebook a comfort? That she, a woman, worked as a scribe is not impossible; female scribes are mentioned in a few inscriptions and literary references.

The cult of the goddess Isis was in ascendancy in the first century in the Greco-Roman world. On Ponza a woman's head from a statue has been found, with a distinctive headdress, and a snake running down the back of it from crown to nape: this is Isis, or one of her priestesses. Isis even reached London, for a second-century souvenir cup has been found there inscribed "from London at the temple of Isis," as well as an altarstone dedicated to the goddess.

About the culture and religion of the ancient British people during the early years of the Roman occupation, very little is known. Many of our popular ideas about the ancient Celts (a word I, like Aubrey, hesitate to use about the people of Britain) are extrapolated from Irish and Welsh writings of the fifth, sixth and subsequent centuries, and not necessarily relevant to the southern part of England in the first century. What I have written is complete speculation; but I have tried to make sure it is not impossible, and fits with what we do know about that time and place. The rituals and ceremonies are my own, although the three mother goddesses have been found in sculpture, especially in southwest England. Plentiful archaeological evidence shows human sacrifice was part of British religious life, but the casting-off of the oarless boat is invented.

Throughout the book, people from the historical record appear: Boudica of Britain, the early Roman Christians Hermas and Grapte, the emperor Domitian, Flavius Clemens, Flavia Domitilla, her steward Stephanus, Cornelia the vestal virgin, Baucylia the nurse, and Paulos and Loukas, known to us as Paul and Luke. But the three Christians Lucius, Zoë, and Dorothea are inventions, as are Glauca and Philemon, the child Lucilius, and the modern woman Aubrey/Avril too.

Christine Whittemore

Acknowledgments

Many people have helped me over the years of researching and writing this book, too many to mention them all. I am very grateful to every single one.

I must thank Debra Leigh Scott, my editor and publisher, and all at Hidden River Arts, for the Eludia Award; and I am so grateful to Debra, to Doug Gordon, and to Miriam Seidel for their work in bringing the book into the world.

My agent, Julia Kenny, has my eternal gratitude for her continued faith in this book; her support and encouragement have meant so much.

Kind encouragers, and helpful readers of various versions, include: Janet Bregman-Taney, Michelle Jacques, Juilene Osborne-McKnight, Penny Ross, Evelyn Sankey, Jan Selving, Michael Steffens, Betsy Tabor, my mother Clare, my siblings Paul, Janie, Simon, Beth, and Mark, and members of my former writing group and book club.

Connie McQuillen Evans helped with the invented Latin text. The professional opinions of Juris Jurjevics, James McCarthy, and Tiffany Murray were extremely useful. I am especially grateful to scholars Professor Alan Bowman and the late Professor Marta Sordi for taking the time to reply to my queries, as well as to scholars on the Elenchus Internet list.

I also thank Carol Varipapa, Barbara Keiser, and all staff of Eastern Monroe Public Library, Stroudsburg, Pennsylvania; Michelle Starr and staff of the Kemp Library at East Stroudsburg University; staff of the Trexler Library at Muhlenberg College, Allentown, Pennsylvania; staff of the Trexler Library at Desales University, Center Valley, Pennsylvania; staff of the Biblioteca Vallicelliana, Chiesa Nuova, Rome; archive document photographer Mario Setter.

My local bookshop, Carroll and Carroll in Stroudsburg, Pennsylvania, was an important resource; Lisa, George, and their richly stocked bookshelves offered information and inspiration.

The Commonwealth of Pennsylvania gave me a Fellowship in Literature Award for poetry in 1998, which I so much appreciate and which made such a difference to my life as a writer.

Special gratitude to my son David Papa, my son Daniel Papa, and my daughter Stephanie Papa for their encouragement, and also because each of them offered insightful readings and feedback that were crucial to the book's evolution.

And above all, I am deeply grateful to my husband, Thomas Papa, for his patience, encouragement, and support, without which this book could not have been written.

Quotations and References

Countless books have been influential, one way or another, in the writing of this one. Suffice it to say my debt of gratitude to all their authors is immense, whether they provided insight into ancient Rome, Iron Age Britain, and early Christianity, or inspired me by making connections and crossing borderlines.

For the epigraphs, permission to reprint has been sought wherever possible. All Aubrey/Avril's epigraphs were originally found in printed books, as she found them. For older printed editions now in the public domain an online reference is occasionally given. All translations from Latin sources are my own unless otherwise stated. Quotations from the Bible are from the public domain World English Bible.

The extract from *The Rings of Saturn* by W.G. Sebald, copyright W.G. Sebald, translated by Michael Hulse, English translation copyright The Harvill Press, 1998, is used by permission of the publisher Random House for the UK, and throughout North America by permission of the Wylie Agency LLC.

The Thomas Traherne (1636/7–1674) quotation is from the opening of his book *Centuries of Meditations* (First Century, 1), from the 1908 edition, edited by Bertram Dobell (1842–1914) (archive.org).

The brief quote by Betsy Wyeth (verbal communication to Richard Meryman) is from p. 421 of *Andrew Wyeth* by Richard Meryman, Copyright © 1996 Richard Meryman. Reprinted by permission of Harper-Collins publishers.

The story about the emperor Gaius "Caligula" and the exiles is from Suetonius, *The Lives of the Caesars*, Book IV, Gaius Caligula, xxviii. Written about 120 AD.

The extract from the tourism leaflet of circa 2000 is my own translation from the Italian.

The Persius quotation (Aulus Persius Flaccus, 34–62 AD) is from the *Satire III*, lines 10–14 in the Latin.

The extract from the letter of Claudia Severa in the Vindolanda tablets is from *Tabulae Vindolandenses II*, by Alan Bowman and David Thomas, 1994, British Museum Press, text number 291, now also on-line (vindolanda.csad.ox.ac.uk—a photograph of the tablet with its writing can also be seen), by permission of the Centre for the Study of Ancient Documents and the British Museum. Claudia Severa wrote this birthday invitation sometime around 100 AD.

The extract from Jerome's letter to Eustochium (Letter CVIII, 7), written in 404 AD to console her for the loss of her mother Paula who had recently died, is taken from the version by Philip Schaff (1819–1893) (Christian Classics Ethereal Library, ccel.org).

The Ovid lines used by Tilla for writing practice are from his poems written in exile, *Tristia ex Ponto*, or *Lamentations from Pontus*, Book 3, viii, lines 7–8 in the Latin. He never returned to Rome.

The extract from the *Ecclesiastical History* (completed by AD 324) by Eusebius of Caesarea (Book III, Chapter 18, 4–5) is from the translation from the Greek of Arthur Cushman McGiffert (1861–1933) (rbedrosian.com).

The extract from Cassius Dio's *Roman History* (Book LXVII, 14, 1–3) is from the Loeb Classical Library, Harvard University Press, translation by Earnest Cary, 1925. Cassius Dio completed his history between AD 229 and his death around AD 235.

The extract from Marta Sordi's *The Christians and the Roman Empire*, © 1983, 1994 Editoriale Jaca Book SpA, English translation Annabel Bedini, is from page 49 of the first paperback edition, published in 1994 by Routledge, and is used by permission.

The extract from *The Emperor Domitian*, by Brian W. Jones, copyright Brian W. Jones, 1992, 1993, Routledge, from page 48 in the 1993 paperback edition, is used by permission.

The extract about the skeleton of the fisherman is from *The Secrets of Vesuvius*, Sara C. Bisel, © 1990, Sara C. Bisel and Family and The Madison Press Limited.

The quotation from Tacitus about the Roman governor Agricola's treatment of the conquered British is from *Agricola* (21). Publius Cornelius Tacitus wrote this book on the career of his father-in-law around AD 98. Agricola was governor of Britannia from AD 77 to 85.

The extract from Chariton's novel *Callirhoe* is reprinted by permission of the publishers and the Trustees of the Loeb Classical Library from *Chariton: Callirhoe* edited by G.P. Goold (LCL 481), Cambridge, Mass.: Harvard University Press, Copyright © 1995 by the President and Fellows of Harvard College. Loeb Classical Library ® is a registered trademark of the President and Fellows of Harvard College. The novel, in Greek, may have been written as early as the middle of the first century AD.

The quotation by Columella about fish ponds is from his *De Re Rustica (On Agriculture)*, Book VIII, Chapter xvii. Lucius Junius Moderatus Columella died around AD 70; his twelve-volume treatise on agriculture was completed a few years before.

The extract from *The Birth of the Codex* by Colin H. Roberts and T.C. Skeat, copyright © 1983 The British Academy, is used by permission of the publisher.

The words about the cloak, books, and parchments are from the Bible, Second Epistle to Timothy, Chapter 4, verse 13.

The extract from a paragraph by John Aubrey (1626–1697) about the fate of old manuscripts comes from a "Digression" in the chapter "Worthies" in Aubrey's *The Natural History of Wiltshire*, unpublished in his lifetime. From the edition by John Britton, 1847 (gutenberg.org).

The passage from Tacitus about the Druids and the destruction of Mona (Anglesey) is from the *Annals*, Book XIV, xxx. Tacitus was still writing this final work in AD 116; the exact date of his death is unknown. The Roman attack on Anglesey under Gaius Suetonius Paulinus took place in AD 60 or 61.

The quotation from Eleanor Farjeon's poem "A Morning Song (for the First day of Spring)," also known as "Morning Has Broken" (written in 1931), from *The Children's Bells*, 1957, Oxford University Press, is used with permission.

The lines from the *Song of Songs*, the book of the Old Testament or Hebrew Bible also known as *The Song of Solomon* and *Canticles*, are from Chapter 2, verse 5.

Extract from "The Ship of Death" by D.H. Lawrence is reprinted by permission of Pollinger Limited (www.pollingerltd.com) on behalf of the estate of Frieda Lawrence Ravagli. The poem was written in late 1929; Lawrence died in March 1930.

The lines by Ovid are again from his *Tristia ex Ponto, Lamentations from Pontus*, Book 1, i, lines 15–16 in the Latin.

The poem by William Blake (1757–1827), "And did those feet in ancient time," also known as "Jerusalem" when sung to Parry's music, is from the preface to his *Milton: A Poem*, written and illustrated between 1804 and 1810.

The words spoken by Nereus to Domitilla occur with slight variations in various retellings of the late medieval legend of Nereus, Achilleus and Domitilla. Here I used *Acta Sanctorum*, Volume 16, by Godfrey Henschen and Daniel von Papebroeck of the Bollandists, published 1680–88. May 12, Saints Nereus, Achilleus and Domitilla, Chapter 1. A later edition is available online at archive.org.

The extract from the *Martyrdom of Polycarp* (translation by Alexander Roberts and James Donaldson, *Ante-Nicene Fathers*, Vol. 1, New York 1899) comes from the letter from the church at Smyrna. Polycarp was killed as an old man c. 160–180 AD. This account was written soon after.

The line from the *Apologeticus*, or *Apology*, of Tertullian (c. 160–225 AD) is from Book L, 13. Quintus Septimus Florens Tertullianus of Carthage is thought to have converted to Christianity around AD 195 and to have written this book in 197 AD.

The extract from R.S. Thomas's poem "The Bright Field" is from *Collected Poems 1945–1990* by R.S. Thomas, Copyright © 1993 R.S. Thomas, by permission of The Orion Publishing Group, London.

The final epigraph, again from Thomas Traherne's *Centuries of Meditations* (Dobell, 1908), is from the Fifth Century, 7.

CPSIA information can be obtained at www.ICGtesting.com
Printed in the USA
LVOW11s1516030915

452709LV00005B/600/P